'You never th

James was at his n
'You never thoug
want to have a baby? His gaze became more
searching as he willed her to conform.

'No, James.' It was painful to deny him when all Jane wanted was to make him happy. 'My career has always meant everything to me. And since we married, James, I have *everything* in the world I want.'

Dear Reader

For many of us, this is the best period of the year—the season of goodwill and celebration—though it can make big demands on your time and pocket, too! Or maybe you prefer to spend these mid-winter months more quietly? Whatever you've got planned, Mills & Boon's romances are always there for you as special friends at the turn of the year: easy, entertaining and comforting reads that are great value for money. Stay warm, won't you!

The Editor

Alexandra Scott was born in Scotland and lived there until she met her husband, who was serving in the British Army, and there followed twenty-five years of travel in the Far East and Western Europe. They then settled in North Yorkshire, and, encouraged (forcefully) by her husband, she began writing the first of some fifty romantic novels which were to be published. Her other interests include gardening and embroidery, and she enjoys the company of her family.

AFTER THE HONEYMOON

BY

ALEXANDRA SCOTT

MILLS & BOON LIMITED
ETON HOUSE   18-24 PARADISE ROAD
RICHMOND   SURREY   TW9 1SR

First published in Great Britain 1992
by Mills & Boon Limited

© Alexandra Scott 1992

Australian copyright 1992
Philippine copyright 1993
This edition 1993

ISBN 0 263 77865 7

Set in Times Roman 11 on 12 pt.
01-9301-46766 C

Made and printed in Great Britain

CHAPTER ONE

SHE half woke, was stretching with unaccustomed languor, when her hands were grasped, pinioned gently but with force on the pillows above her head, then the drugging, intoxicating brush of lips began. 'No!' The moment her mouth was freed she made her protest, but it came out as a more appreciative sound, a lingeringly appreciative, 'Mmm!' Whatever she had meant, it was highly satisfactory that her true wishes were so correctly interpreted, the directions to the contrary so entirely disregarded. He even anticipated her intention to flutter open her eyelids by feathering them with kisses, delicate as a butterfly.

Unbelievable, incredible—the most over-active, unpredictable imagination could have done nothing to prepare her for this, such delicious wildness, such obsession, intensity rising inside her with such irresistible force . . .

One of her hands was released and his arm moved beneath her, circling her waist, pulling her body up and into contact with his. She gasped, at the same time reaching for the nape of his neck, increasing the pressure of his lips which were again teasing hers. After a few moments he drew back, her eyelids drifted open and she was looking up into the eyes that had caused her such trouble on that very first day. Almost black, but they were still brown, dark dreamy brown, glinting with the most unexpected amber flecks. Right now they were sparkling with something close to amusement, though on that first occasion they had blazed with anger. Just over a week ago, that was! Who would have believed she could behave so impetuously, and yet . . . ?

'Tell me about yourself.' He was smiling, at both of them, not solely at her. 'Tell me the story of your life.'

'What——?' Automatically her lips curved in response; as it had been since they had first got together, her heart was hammering so fiercely that she knew he must be aware of it. 'What exactly do you want to know?'

'Oh, just everything—where you went to school, who was your best friend, where you went on holiday when you were a girl and . . . oh, just everything. In detail.' His mouth was moving against hers again, her reply was smothered as they were swept away by something much more urgent.

'Breakfast?' He looked up much later as she sauntered out on to the veranda, the expression in his eyes bringing the flutter back into her throat and a wave of heat to her skin which raising her hand to push back the fall of dark silky hair did little to disguise.

'Sounds like a good idea.' She smiled then, a long leisurely intimate exchange which neither wanted to curtail. 'Only,' she ran the tip of her tongue over her lips, amused at how provocative she had suddenly become, 'I think first of all I'll have a shower.'

'Mmm.' He raised his coffee-cup and sipped, his eyes above the rim still intent. 'Is that by any chance an invitation?' And he grinned in wicked appreciation as colour scorched her cheeks again.

'I thought,' it was strange for Jane to feel vulnerable, and instinct dictated she take a more positive line, 'I thought you'd already had a shower.' She looked at his still damp hair.

'I won't melt if I have another.' He got up from his chair then, took a step towards her, folding her tenderly against him, his hand moving caressingly over the thin silk of his pyjama top worn as a robe. 'But I mustn't tease you, my sweet. Since this situation is one I know you're not used to, I've decided——'

'It's one I could oh, so easily become used to.' Some of her normal self-assurance was flowing back.

'But not too quickly, eh?' For a minute he held her away from him, taking in the mane of glossy hair tumbling to her shoulders, the wide green eyes, the perfect curve of cheeks and lips. 'Not too quickly.' His voice was low, intense. 'There's nothing about you I feel I'll ever become used to.'

'But then,' with a flirtatious little shrug she escaped, looking round invitingly as she made for the bathroom, 'you know very little about me, James Barnard.' Silk slithered down over one shoulder.

'That's why...' He closed the door by leaning against it, watching as she tossed the garment in the direction of the chair. 'That's why I've decided we mustn't waste a single moment. And you can begin to tell me the story of your life while I soap your back.'

Much later that day, Jane looked down at the dark head on the pillow beside her. Surprised by the wave of uncontrolled emotion that swept through her, she forced herself to suppress the urge to reach out and brush the ebony-black hair back from his forehead. There was a tiny frown on his face—it was as if he too was bewildered by all that had happened in the seven days since they had left Heathrow.

Seven days since Jane had set out on what promised to be a fairly ordinary restful holiday in the Caribbean, but it had turned out to be neither. She smiled at her own tendency to blush as the thought struck with some force. Neither ordinary nor restful!

She had noticed him before he as much as glanced at her—he could protest about that fact as much as he liked. He had arrived late in the departure lounge, his air of total self-confidence in no way diminished by the way the pretty young stewardess was flapping about him, clearing a way through the regulations as if he were minor royalty.

Tall—from the cover of dark glasses and a copy of *Beaumonde* magazine Jane took note—ridiculously handsome, which put him out of bounds as far as her own interest was concerned. Always she had found handsome men too aware of the fact, too used to having their own way ever to feel attracted by them, and this one... But even if she was to admit to the tiny *frisson* of excitement in her stomach, she was determined it would have not the slightest effect on her attitude.

And certainly—recollection brought a gurgle of laughter to her throat now, instantly stilled lest she disturb him—certainly she hadn't thrown that gin and tonic down his neck on the plane simply to secure his attention. Although it was useless to pretend it had not been done in the most abrupt and forceful way possible. One moment he had been quietly reading a paperback novel, the next he was on his feet and practically spitting his fury.

'I'm so sorry,' just then she was wishing a hole would appear in the fuselage so she could make an emergency exit, 'so terribly sorry! I...'

'Are you in the habit,' he snarled, his dark eyes flashing furiously, 'of throwing drinks over everyone?'

'No.' Her voice shook a little; being the participant in such a public scene was not her idea of a great start to a restful holiday. 'I'm sorry,' she indicated the mother and child just making their way back into the seats adjoining hers, 'my neighbours had to get out and I thought it would make things easier for them...'

'Easier to blame them, you mean.'

'That's not what I was going to say.' There was just so much she was prepared to let him get away with, and that point was approaching rapidly. 'But I suppose you were aware of some turbulence. I was simply standing there, holding the glass for safety, when we dropped into that air pocket. You don't imagine I did it on purpose, I hope?'

By this time the stewardess was brushing him down with a cloth, uttering the cooing noises designed to soothe but which Jane found indescribably irritating.

'I'm not sure.' With a final glare, a look in his eyes which she took to indicate that such ploys were not unknown to him, he turned away, shook his book to emphasise that it had not escaped the deluge and resumed his seat, leaving a seething Jane with no choice but to do the same.

So she sat, watching the arrogant top of that dark head, her mind busy with the various refined forms of torture which would have suited the occasion. Self-satisfied, smug, pompous—he had all the qualities she would have expected to find in a man like that. The kind who would snap his fingers and have women jumping through hoops. She lay back in her seat, eyes closed to shut out the aggravation...and besides, he hadn't seemed to notice her. Not as a woman, she meant, and she was used to being noticed. She might as well have saved herself the effort of putting together the perfect travel outfit, for all the attention he paid her.

Tan mini-skirt in softest suede—Jane ran the palm of her hand down to check that it was still there. And visible. She knew it made the best of her long slender legs. Pure silk shirt in a colour that just missed matching her eyes and a dashing waistcoat checked in tan and green.

She sighed deeply, wishing the journey was behind them and she was settled. She just hoped he wasn't going to be a guest in the same hotel. It would be intolerable if they were forced to spend the holiday glowering at each other across the restaurant. Anyway—she closed her eyes with determination—another two hours to go before they landed at their destination; she might as well try to forget the episode until then.

There was a slight crush round the reception desk in the very plushy Ocean Bay Hotel as they all waited for room allocation. With a smile Jane stepped back, giving way to Carla, her neighbour on the flight and the indirect cause of the incident. 'She looks exhausted.' Jane put out a hand to touch the child who was clinging on to her mother's neck.

'And that makes two of us.' Carla smiled wearily. 'The times I've promised myself I wouldn't take flights that arrive in the middle of the night, but I still do it. And,' she dropped a kiss on the little girl's head, 'she was up at the crack of dawn—you know what kids are like . . .'

Which of course she didn't, Jane thought with something approaching relief. It was bad enough coping with one's own troubles on these long-haul flights, but having to look after a young child as well . . .

But at last it was her turn. She took the key, listened to instructions which seemed to relate to some food being brought to the bedroom and took a step backwards, feeling her high heel grinding into someone's instep. 'Oh, I'm so sorr——' She whirled round, but the words dried on her lips as she looked into the features briefly contorted with pain, her apology at once replaced by wholly irrational indignation. 'Do you always creep up behind people like that?'

'And here was I,' it was a drawl, supercilious and sarcastic, 'thinking you were going to apologise. Again. This time for trying to bore a hole through my foot.'

Speechless, Jane saw him being handed his key, then they were being ushered together towards the lift, two bellboys dealing with their heavy bags. She simmered at what she decided was the affected way he limped, refused to be softened by the beginnings of a smile which she caught from the corner of her eye as they were whisked upwards.

The lift stopped and, still angry, she reached for the bag, which as well as passport and tickets held a fair weight of bits and pieces, several paperback books, a magazine, an assortment of skin preparations, and swung the strap on to her shoulder. Naturally, at the same instant he decided to lift a small case and managed to get his hand right in the way. Her bag struck with some force, she tried not to notice, but colour rushed into her skin.

He stood there, rubbing his hand, staring down at her, and there was no way she could now complain about not being noticed. She was subjected to a very slow, intense scrutiny before he said a word, then his tone was considering rather than complaining. 'You do seem to have it in for me, don't you?'

She swept from the lift and stood waiting for the boy to open the door of room 306. 'Don't flatter yourself!' And it wasn't until she was alone in her room that she realised he had been putting his key into the lock of 307.

She just wouldn't stand for it. In the morning, after she'd had a decent night's sleep and felt rested, she would insist that the hotel move her to another room. It was impossible to have him just through the wall listening to her every move. Every time she had a shower, when she flushed the loo, for heaven's sake, he would know what she was about. And though the balconies seemed well screened, it would be comparatively easy for him, if he were so inclined, to...

She turned as someone knocked at the door, and it opened when the smiling bellboy appeared with a tray of food which he placed on a small table and then left. Jane wasn't really hungry, but she enjoyed the chilled soup with a bread roll, left the omelette and salad but found the slice of pawpaw refreshing. And then nothing, absolutely nothing in her life had ever been as inviting as that wide bed, cool cotton sheets...

She slept well and deeply. Even the thought of that dark head lying on the pillow just a foot from hers wasn't enough to keep her awake, and when she woke she found much of her irritation had vanished. She wasn't even certain she wanted to persist with her intention to move rooms. Certainly—she wandered on to the balcony—she would be reluctant to sacrifice this view. She leaned on the rail, entranced by the vista of cloudless sky, aquamarine sea studded with islands like tiny green pincushions, waves breaking in a lazy frill on pure white sand. No, there was no way she meant to give up her room, but if—if a certain person irritated her just once more she might insist that the management move him.

The idea lifted her spirits still further. She filled her lungs with the soft fragrant air and turned back into the room, singing gently to herself as she began to get ready. The bikini was good. That, she approved as she twisted and turned in front of the long mirror, was one of the great benefits of working as a fashion reporter for a magazine like *Beaumonde*. Wickedly expensive clothes, used in features, were often available to the staff of the Beaumont publishing group at a fraction of their true price.

Such as this perfectly plain designer bikini. Black Lycra edged with green, the top was much more substantial than most, but in some ways it was more

eyecatching, and certainly its clinging lines did
nothing to hide Jane's very feminine shape. Briefs
not too brief but cut away at the sides, exagger-
ating the length of her already long legs. Mmm,
yes, she decided, and topped by the matching shift,
see-through cotton in green splashed with black, it
was perfect for breakfast round the pool as adver-
tised in the holiday brochure.

Jane slipped her feet into high wedges, picked up
her bag, then with a little grin, removed about half
of the contents. No sense in weighing herself down
with a lot of useless clutter; one book was as much
as she was likely to read at a time. She had already
planned her day of total leisure interspersed with
one or two brief dips in the sea. But first of all,
she felt really hungry and ready for whatever the
hotel provided by way of breakfast.

Her finger was still on the lift bell when she heard
another door open, then it closed, and she knew
without looking up—the prickle of apprehension
on the nape of her neck was confirmation—exactly
whose shadow fell on her.

'Good morning.' Without as much as a glance
she stepped into the lift, her heart hammering so
violently that she barely heard his reply. She just
saw the long finger reach out for the row of buttons,
noticed the heavy gold watch on his wrist, the
sprinkle of dark hair on strong forearms.

'Reception?' Something in his manner com-
pelled her to look at him. She was immediately disconcerted by the expression of amusement and was

relieved she had had the foresight to wear her dark glasses.

'Please.' Cool as ice. She stared ahead. As if the bronze-coloured doors could wipe away the picture of him—sand-coloured chinos, feet thrust into thongs, shirt open to the waist showing a wide expanse of dark skin. And why should she be pleased that there was no sign of the gold chains which adorned so many male necks these days?

'Have you forgiven me yet?' The voice was deep, she had already registered that, deep and pretty well as attractive as the man himself.

'Forgiven you?' Her tone, deliberately blank, implied that she had not until that instant thought of him. She raised her eyebrows with what she hoped was discouraging coolness.

'*You* know,' he shrugged, no longer pretending to hide his amusement. 'For getting in the way of that gin and tonic you threw around on the flight. Then for insinuating my instep under that stiletto you were wearing.'

'Haven't you forgotten...' her rippling response of laughter was becoming difficult to control '...there was the incident in the lift?'

'Yes, that too. Assault with a weighted handbag. You're not a female politician, are you? If so, are you asking for that to be taken into consideration?'

Now there was no chance, or point, of suppressing the grin. 'Might as well, I suppose.' When she looked directly at him she blinked, startled by the blatant admiration and interest in his eyes, startled too by her own instant flare of response. He *was* an attractive man, and after all, she *was* on holiday, and...

'Then, as it's obviously a first offence, I'll be lenient and sentence you to spending the morning skin-diving with me.'

'Wait a minute.' They emerged into the coolness of the foyer, crossed in the direction of the restaurant. 'I thought in the beginning the implication was that you were in the wrong, and my indulgence was being sought. How come, then, I'm the one being sentenced?'

He held open the heavy tinted glass door for her, then as they hesitated, waiting for attention, he shrugged, extending his palms upwards in a gesture of surrender. 'Have it your own way.' He glanced up as the waiter approached. 'I think we'd like to eat outside.' Masterful, as she'd already guessed, but now it was less irritating than she could have imagined. 'Rooms 306 and 307.' His hand was on her elbow as they walked through wide open windows and on to the shady veranda where tables under huge fringed parasols were set around the pool.

As she said good morning to one or two people she had spoken to on the flight, Jane felt the colour rise in her face, especially when she saw Carla's expressively raised eyebrow commenting on her companion.

'Well?' They were seated, pink linen napkins spread over their knees, glasses of freshly squeezed orange in front of them, before he returned to his original theme. 'Are you going to sit in judgement?'

'Mmm.' She sipped, looking away from him, out over the bay, still reluctant to admit to herself how excited and stimulated she felt in this man's company. 'I'm trying to decide what would be appropriate, and I think what you suggest might be punishment enough—you see, I've never done any skin-diving before.' She flicked her lashes, looking down at her plate for a moment before covertly returning her attention to him. 'I can swim, though. I can do the width of the pool at home and I once managed a whole length. But I've never tried that again.'

For just a moment she was amused by his look of consternation, but it was wiped away almost at once, as he grinned quite suddenly. 'Then,' he reached out for the coffee-pot and filled two cups, 'it looks as if there's quite a lot I can teach you. But maybe it would be best to start by introducing ourselves. I'm James Barnard.'

'Jane Wyatt.' Ridiculous to feel so self-conscious, like a naïve teenager. She welcomed the diversion as rolls arrived with plates of butter resting on bowls of ice, a selection of preserves and fruit.

'Somehow,' he had very white teeth which bit decisively into the bread, 'I hadn't thought of you as a Jane, but now I've decided it suits you.'

'And I hadn't thought of you,' the sharp little gibe was a help in hiding her reactions, 'as James or as anything else.'

He looked at her, eyebrows raised, a long leisurely tender survey which had her insides quivering. 'Liar,' he said in that low throbbing drawl, and at the same time he lifted her hand from the table and held it cradled in his. 'Liar,' he repeated, and she knew it was the most possessive statement that had ever been made.

He was a persuasive teacher, she found, though there was a certain undisguised relief when he found that she wasn't quite the novice she had pretended, as she confessed to a limited number of snorkelling expeditions on the Greek islands.

'You're certainly a much better swimmer than you let me think.' They had surfaced after the first brief foray along the reef, parking their gear on the raft, drifting idly on the current. 'In fact, not bad at all for a woman.'

'Mmm.' Jane refused to take the bait, amazed at how contented she felt simply floating on the surface, gazing up at the cloudless sky. 'Exactly what I was going to say about you.'

'That I'm not bad for a woman?' He grabbed her shoulders threateningly. 'Because I'm quite prepared to point out your fundamental mistake.'

With a lithe little backward flip she freed herself from him, went down through crystal-clear water, picked up a smooth round pebble which she tossed lightly towards him when she surfaced. 'For a man.' She returned to what they had been saying. 'You're not a bad swimmer for a man.'

He grinned. A couple of powerful strokes brought him towards her, and they trod water while staring into each other's eyes. Jane felt every nerve in her body tingle with pleasure.

Everything about him seemed designed to catch the eye and hold it—the dark suntanned skin, the crisp triangle of chest hair, water droplets clinging with all the glittering attraction of diamonds, sable hair slicked against his skull like a cap, eyes gleaming, taking no trouble to hide the attraction he felt. 'Ready to dive again?' He waited, and when she didn't answer he grinned as if aware of the cause of her hesitation. 'Yes?' he prompted.

'Yes. Oh, yes!' she replied instantly, and with a fervency she regretted as another example of naïveté.

But it was wonderful to be introduced to the fascinating world of diving along even such a small reef as this, with tiny fish in darting shoals of brilliant colour, plants waving elegantly in the stir of the tide. Once a large shape threw a menacing shadow over them and she knew a thrill of real terror until James caught her hand reassuringly, pulling her against him as the huge ray sailed past above their heads.

'That,' when at last they surfaced and heaved themselves on to the raft she reached for her towel and draped it round her shoulders, 'was simply mind-blowing! Thank you.' Aware of his eyes, she couldn't stop the rise of colour in her cheeks. 'Thank you, James, for taking me.'

'It was a pleasure.' He rubbed a hand across his chest, making her still more aware of him. 'It was by no means the punishment you threatened.'

'Mmm. Pity.' Deliberately provocative, she began to towel her hair. 'That rather defeats the whole intention, wouldn't you say?'

'In that case, maybe you'll be able to think of something else, something that really fits the crime. Come on, then,' his manner changed abruptly, 'I'm starving after all that exercise.' He began to collect their things and threw them into the small motorboat which had brought them out. 'What do you say to a long cool drink before lunch?'

'Sounds like a great idea.' Jane pulled the shift over her damp bikini, accepted his offer of a steadying hand and jumped lightly aboard.

'Then,' he pulled the starting cord and sat in the bows, his hand on the tiller as the engine jumped into life, 'you can begin to tell me all about yourself.'

'So that's it, then, is it?' They had eaten a delicious meal of steamed clams with bread and butter, were finishing dishes of fruit salad, sipping low-alcohol white wine, when James sat back in his chair with a sigh of contentment. 'That's as much as you're prepared to divulge. Jane Wyatt, twenty-seven and with no ties—I find that hard to believe—out on holiday on her own as a relief from a frantic season in the rag trade.'

'Well,' she pursed her lips in assumed displeasure, 'I'm not sure that Beaumont Publishing would approve your description of their exclusive premises, but yes, that's about it. And alone because my friend went down with chickenpox.'

'I'd have said twenty-four rather than twenty-seven.'

'You would?' Jane raised a dark slender eyebrow, refusing to let him know how eager she was for his compliments.

'Maybe even twenty-three,' he grinned mischievously, then quite abruptly got to his feet, holding out a hand which she took without thinking. 'And now I'm going to prescribe bed for you. You're still jet-lagged and you've had more than enough sun for one day.'

He led her across the terrace and through the restaurant. Jane waved casually at some people who were still eating, thankful that no one could guess how feverishly her heart was beating against her ribs. She had been in this very situation before and had always found it easy to deal with, but now all her confidence in repelling advances had simply evaporated, her will had gone.

They reached their corridor. James took her key, seeming not to notice how much her hand was shaking, put it in the lock and pushed open the door. 'You look all in, my sweet.' He bent his head, barely touching her lips with his. 'Have a peaceful siesta. And if you're good, I might buy you a proper drink before dinner.'

And before she knew what was happening she found herself inside the small hallway, the outer door closed. And she was alone. No decision to make. It was difficult to know whether she should laugh or cry. But in the end she gave way to another quite overwhelming need. She lay down on the bed and slept.

It seemed taken for granted that they would share a table in the restaurant, and they were shown to one in the arch of an open window with the sound of water lapping just a few yards away and the spectacular canopy of stars above.

Jane was conscious of looking her best, and if confirmation were needed it was offered in the interested glances as she passed other guests. The calf-length skirt she was wearing was splashed in shades of rose and green and topped by a silk camisole supported by narrow straps. A wide belt drew attention to her slender waist, and gilt earrings tinkled as she moved her head.

She had lavished care and attention on her hair. Lots of conditioner had left it fragrant and shining, drifting about her shoulders like skeins of filmy silk. Lightest of touches with make-up—her skin was already taking on a peachy glow—some goldy-bronze eyeshadow, lipstick that enhanced the soft vulnerability of the mouth and a final dusting of powder. She was generous with her spray of light flowery scent, and when there was a crisp knock at the door she whirled away from her reflection in her rush to answer it.

One hand extended to the wall supported him, but he straightened when the door was opened and stood there simply looking at her for an endless heady minute. Then he smiled, put out a finger and gently touched her hair. 'Ready?'

Jane nodded, unable to speak, then turned back to pick up her purse, but his image was branded on to her psyche, immovable even if that was what she wanted. Dark trousers, black slip-on shoes and white cotton shirt was a maroon striped tie. She noticed, approvingly, that he wore heavy gold cuff-links set with some kind of polished stones and about him there was the aroma of some subtle faintly exotic cologne.

'It's a pity...' When they had eaten, it seemed natural for them to wander along the beach. Jane raised her eyes to look at the sky, at the same time enjoying the feel of warm sand in her toes. For just a moment she was barely aware that James had spoken, the night itself was so enchanting, dark sapphire sky strewn with stars, palm trees dark cut-outs against the sparkling ocean. 'I've got to move on tomorrow.'

'Mmm. It's so beautiful!'

'You haven't heard a word I've been saying.' He turned her to him, fingers pressing into the bare skin of her shoulders. 'Does it mean so little to you?' The tone of suppressed emotion got through to her in a way that the words failed to do.

'What?' There was a sudden change of attitude, one moment perfect content and the next, a distinct *frisson* of uncertainty. 'What did you say, James?'

'I was saying,' amused tolerance was now diluting his irritation, 'how sorry I am that I have to move on tomorrow.'

'Move on?' Fear clutched at her, though she couldn't just then have diagnosed the emotion. 'Wh-what on earth do you mean?'

'I mean,' he spoke moodily, releasing her, turning to resume their walk along the beach, kicking at the sand, 'I mean that I booked into Ocean Bay for just two nights. After that I arranged to move to the other side of the island. My company has a bungalow there, and——'

'You're going?' The truth was like a slap on the face to her. 'Leaving?'

'Yes. But you needn't be on your own.' Here there was a hint of sarcasm. 'There's at least two men in there,' he jerked his head back in the direction of the hotel, 'who've been looking at you hungrily since we arrived.'

'Yes.' Jane blinked away tears that surprised her with their suddenness, tried to make a joke. 'If I'd thought, I could have drenched one of them with gin and tonic. The short fat one, I think, don't you, rather than the thin weedy one?'

'He's the one you prefer, is he? Maybe when we go back you can trip on the veranda and send him flying into the pool. With any luck he might be unable to swim.'

'James,' his manner made her giggle, 'you sound...you can't be jealous.'

'Can't I?'

'But he has no chin and very little hair, and...' Turning, she put her hands on his shoulders and looked up into his face, subduing an urge to smooth away the frown from his forehead.

'None of that matters if you fancy him even a little.'

'I'm not sure if I ought to be flattered or insulted. Even if I hadn't met you... I mean, if I hadn't had the presence of mind to anaesthetise you with alcohol so I could have my way with you, do you seriously think I'd have wanted to spend my time with him? I imagine his idea of an exciting evening would be a game of dominoes.'

'Don't you believe it, my sweet. All men when they look at you have the same idea of what would constitute an exciting evening. And dominoes wouldn't come into it. Base instincts don't vary much when a desirable woman is——'

'Is that how you see me?' It was a breathy little question, as she leaned towards him, her hands linking about his neck.

'If you don't know it then I'm afraid I'm losing my touch.' James sighed, smiled, smoothed her hair back from her face. She could feel his breath stirring against her skin, sensuous and beguiling. 'I want you with the kind of wildness I never expected to experience. I'm mad about you, Jane Wyatt, and I can't imagine what we're going to do about it.'

He kissed her then. Not the brief detached kind of caress which she had found so frustrating but with a tender exploration that caused a slight intake of sound in her throat. Her eyelids drifted closed, darkness swirled about her as she gave herself up to the unimaginable pleasure of his mouth against hers.

'James...' She was trembling and clinging, her legs all at once incapable of supporting her.

'Jane.' His breathing was light and quick, one hand circled her neck, the other tilted her face up to his. 'Jane,' it was close to a groan, 'Jane, my darling. I'm afraid... the truth is, it sounds mad when we've known each other only a few hours, I think—no, I don't think, I *know* I've fallen in love with you. And I'm hoping, quite desperately I'm hoping, that maybe you feel the same way...'

That... *That* was how it had all happened less than a week ago.

Jane reached out again for her paperback novel. She really ought to try to finish it, but when she saw how few pages she had read she shook her head disapprovingly. Only when a hand, a slender dark masculine hand, came out and took it from her, she looked round with a coquettish grin and slid further down into the bed.

'You realise, don't you, that we have just a few more days of all this?' James waved a hand round the luxurious bedroom. 'What do you say we contact our various employers, say we've been struck down with a bug and need an extra week to recover?'

'Oh, yes? And what sort of bug—did you mean to specify? The love bug, perhaps.'

'Only if you must be truthful.'

'I don't think it's absolutely necessary to give chapter and verse. I'll let them know I mean to stay on a few extra days—I don't suppose they'll give me the boot.'

'And if they do, would it matter so much? I quite like to think of my——'

'Not matter?' In mock indignation Jane pushed away from her. 'Of course it matters! Didn't I tell you my big ambition is to be given the top job of fashion editor, if Mrs Devere decides to give up? I haven't put in all those extra hours, slaved for so many years, to miss out on the big one, James Barnard!'

'You should have told me.' Masterfully he pushed her back, catching her earlobe in his teeth. 'I had no idea I'd fallen in love with such an ambitious woman.'

'As I said, there's so much about me you don't know.'

'All I need to know is that you love me as much as I love you.'

'Haven't I shown that I do?' Now she was intent, serious. 'Do you think I would have married you otherwise, James Barnard? I married you because I love you, and I mean to spend the rest of my life showing you how much.'

CHAPTER TWO

'YOU know——' James came up behind Jane as she was standing in front of a mirror combing her hair, sweeping it softly into the elegant french pleat which she preferred for work. He leaned forward, his cheek touching hers, eyes glinting with brilliant persuasion. 'You know,' one finger curled a wisp of hair at the nape of her neck, 'you really *ought* to have called in and told them you needed a few more days...' He explored the length of her silk-covered spine, each disc examined with tingling intimacy.

'James!' It was a breathless little protest; her clear green eyes widened in alarm, and she reached up and removed the two hairpins she was holding in her mouth, stabbing them securely in the glossy hair. 'James, don't you dare.'

'Don't dare what?' With one swift move he had his hands on her waist, whirling her round to face him, moulding her slender body closely against his. 'Don't dare...what?' he demanded, his mouth against her skin causing all kinds of distraction, havoc to her senses.

'Don't dare,' with a little sigh she relaxed, enjoying the game at least as much as he did and for the moment prepared to indulge both of them, 'don't dare do this.' Her eyes drifted closed, she raised her hands and laced her fingers through the ebony darkness of his hair. 'Nor this.' She drew his mouth into contact with her own, surprised by the strength of her leaping response which was almost as fierce as his. Then her lips parted and she allowed a little moan to escape.

It would be so easy—easy to give in to the clamour of her senses, to allow him to do what he was doing right now, to slide the covering from her shoulders and... It was what she longed for above anything, but...

'James!' It was sheer panic. With a tiny unexpected twist she broke from him, laughing back at his expression of exaggerated frustration. '*Please* don't!' She backed away from him as he reached out for her again. 'I'm asking you to *help* me, not hinder.'

Nevertheless, she knew she was setting out to be deliberately provocative, in the languid way she tossed aside the wrap, letting it slither from the bed with a silky whisper, in the way she stood for a long moment in her black underskirt, narrow straps, lace bra top designed to persuade and allure. Then in one smooth move she stepped into the black pencil skirt, adjusted it so the high slit was centre front, and pulled up the zip. The scoop-necked wool jumper was next, and she eased herself into it, taking great care that her hair should be undisturbed, and all the time she was aware of the dark lounging figure, hawklike as he watched her every move.

She began a soft little humming, then stopped, breathless for no reason she wanted to confront at that moment. 'Darling,' she made a tiny pleading gesture, palms upwards, '*please* help me.'

'So,' he grinned, 'what am I doing.'

'*You* know. And I must—I *must* get to work today!'

'Must you?' Both his tone and manner were all at once more sombre than she had expected. She was taken aback and gave a perplexed little laugh.

'Of course I must—you know that. I can't risk going back to Beaumont's to find they've promoted my assistant.'

'Would that be such a ... disaster?'

'To me it would.' Annoyed now where a moment before she had been all warmth and indulgence, Jane turned back to the glass and began swiftly, efficiently to apply the light make-up which would see her through to lunchtime. She darted an accusing look as he turned away. 'A complete disaster.' The broad, still sunburned shoulders were shrugged into a shirt. 'Wouldn't it annoy you, if you found yourself in a situation like that?'

It was a moment before he answered. The long dark fingers dealt efficiently with buttons and gold cufflinks, and when he spoke his tone was reflective. 'You know, I don't think it would—but then I've never thought of myself as particularly ambitious.'

That made her laugh, it was so blatantly ridiculous. 'Oh, James! Men don't become senior oil executives at the age of thirty-five unless there's ambition lurking there somewhere.'

'Ah, but that...' His mood had relaxed a little; he smiled at her in the glass as he pulled up the dark maroon tie, stretching his neck slightly, running a finger under the collar before reaching for his jacket. 'Sheer brilliance, wouldn't you say?' Taking up a silver-backed brush, he stroked it through his hair. 'Brilliance rather than ambition?' He raised a rakish self-mocking eyebrow.

'And modesty, don't forget.'

'That too, of course.' As he held her jacket for her he dropped a kiss on the nape of her neck. 'But in any event, the two cases are entirely different.'

'Different?' Jane frowned at her reflection, then leaned forward to touch her lips with a little more of the pinky-beige lipstick. 'How? Please explain, just how are they different?'

'It's not something you can explain—besides, it's so basic it should need no definition, and... Ssh!' As she was about to speak he put his fingers to her mouth. 'Ssh!' His eyes were sparkling with mischievous amusement and in spite of herself she felt her flare of irritation fade. 'You still insist on going back to work today?' Her brief nod of confirmation brought a profound sigh. 'Well, in that case, we'd best be on our way. I'll drop you off before I do anything else. Anyway, you know I'm dying to meet the wonderful Lottie; I've heard so much about her.'

'Yes—well, you and Lottie might have a lot in common,' she told him.

'We both adore you, is that what you mean?'

'That's not what I mean, as you know. But you might find you share the same antediluvian attitude towards married women in the workplace. Lottie makes no secret of her preference for the domestic life.'

'Oh? Is that so?' James spoke mildly, then grinned. 'Would it be considered antediluvian if I were to say you look wonderful when you're angry?'

'Corny, rather. And I'm not angry, just rather surprised.'

'Irritated, then.' But his eyes narrowed as he watched her putting a few final touches to her appearance, and as she picked up her handbag he put his hands on her shoulders so he was behind her as they looked into the glass. 'But it doesn't alter the fact that you're a very beautiful woman, Mrs Barnard.'

'Am I?' Limpid green eyes searched his. She reached up a finger and traced the line of his jaw.

'You must know it.' His voice was deeper, lower. 'But tell you what, if we don't go *now*, I think it's highly unlikely that Beaumont's are going to see their favourite fashion reporter today.'

A faint smile lingered on Jane's face as they made their stop-and-start way through London's rush-hour traffic. It was bewildering to think that four short weeks ago they had each been unaware of the other's existence, and now they were married, the honeymoon was over and they were settling down to married life. She would never have believed it would happen like that to her, fairy-tales were not her thing, but now she could hardly deny them, and she was happier than she had ever believed possible. Tired too, of course. No one had ever told her about that side of it, but there was no mystery as to the reason. Delicate pink touched her cheeks, her lips tightened primly and she sighed. She was so idyllically happy.

'If you turn left here, James,' she came back to the present with a bump, 'staff parking is just round this corner and down the ramp into the basement.' Now that she was back in the familiar surroundings she felt her heart begin to flutter as if she were afraid. As James held open the door for her he seemed to gauge her mood instantly.

'Nervous?' Eyes, voice, touch, all were tender.

She nodded, adjusting the white silk scarf knotted at her throat. 'Maybe just a little.'

'Then would you prefer to go in on your own?'

'Don't you dare!' She twisted her fingers in his. 'I need all the support I can get. Besides, I'm determined to show you off. I've got to produce some reason for going so completely bananas. Far be it from me to want to undermine your modesty, but . . . I want to watch all the other girls drool over you—it was one of my main aims in marrying you, after all.' And when the lift doors opened a few minutes later they stepped out together, no one would have been able to guess just how feverishly they had been entwined between the basement and the third floor.

'Well,' beamed Lottie as she bustled about with the coffee machine and cups, 'it certainly caused a bit of a sensation, your news.' Jane was sitting on the corner of her desk swinging long legs, while James lounged back in a chair watching her with a look of faintly sardonic appreciation. 'James...' Lottie handed him his cup, offered sugar and cream before she sat down behind her typewriter. 'The whole place was buzzing with speculation. And you say,' she sipped, eyebrows raised in astonishment, 'you really are saying you hadn't met till you got on the plane?'

'She threw herself at me, Lottie.' James's eyes were firmly on his wife's. 'Forced herself on my attention.'

'Really?' Warm brown eyes sparkled behind the gold-rimmed spectacles. 'But it doesn't seem as if you needed a great deal of encouragement.'

'Thank you, Lottie. He accuses me of throwing a glass of gin and tonic over him.'

'Oh, dear.' Lottie was clearly enjoying herself. 'It does seem a rather desperate way to go about things.'

'Her parents,' James drained his cup and put it down on the desk, signalling his intention to leave, 'flew out to try to stop the wedding, did you know that? But I, on the other hand, had no one to look out for me. A lamb to the slaughter, that was me.'

'How romantic!' Ignoring the implication of what he said, Lottie sighed. 'It must have been the most romantic wedding ever.' She looked dreamily into the mid-distance for a few moments, oblivious of the amused glances passing between the other two. 'Your mother said you'd taken some wonderful photographs. Have you brought any with you, Jane?'

'By chance...' Jane produced a large wallet from her handbag and passed it across the desk. 'And we have a video of the whole ceremony—we'll let you see it some time soon.'

'Lovely dress.' Lottie spoke a little wistfully.

Feeling guilty at her friend's obvious distress at missing the wedding, although it had clearly not been possible for Lottie to attend, Jane rushed into speech.

'Yes, well... Anyway, there are some very fashionable boutiques in the Caribbean, it's not all palm trees and beaches. It was ivory lawn with insets of lace at the waist—you can see better in this one—and just above the hem. Frangipani in my hair,' Jane adopted a mocking pose, 'and for the posy. Oh, and...' her left hand was extended to show the Victorian setting of her emerald and diamond ring, 'James bought me this in New York—we came home that way.'

'Gorgeous.' Lottie admired without a trace of envy. 'It looks just perfect for you.'

'But now,' James rose and moved to the door, 'I'd better get out of the way and leave you to your mutual admiration. I think I'll just drop into the office for half an hour and then I'll go up to your flat and pick up some more of your things. That's how,' he explained to Lottie, 'we've spent our time since we got home, ferrying boxes back and forward.'

'Ah, so you're going to be living in...'

'In James's flat,' Jane finished for her. 'It's much bigger than mine. Not quite so convenient for the Underground, but still...'

'I'll be off, then. Goodbye, Lottie, you will come round one night and we'll show you how to get married on video.' James dropped a quick kiss on Jane's cheek. 'See you tonight, then.'

'Yes, I'll make my own way home.' She looked at him, most reluctant to see him go. 'I'll just walk with you as far as the lift.'

But before they could reach the office door it opened, and a man stood there, hesitating when he saw James. 'Oh, Arthur.' Instantly confused by the heat in her skin, Jane tried to inject some pleasure into her manner while wishing she could have postponed this meeting until she'd had time to have a private word. 'I'm so glad you came. James,' her blush showed no sign of fading, 'I'd like you to meet a very good friend. Arthur Davis is our financial director, and... Arthur, you'll have heard our news.' She bit her lip. 'James and I were married when we were on holiday.'

'Of course.' Arthur blinked behind his glasses and smiled. 'Quite a sensation you caused. So unexpected, but, of course, best wishes.'

Hard to avoid comparisons as they shook hands, the one so tall, straight and dark, the other stooping, balding. No one would have guessed how few years separated them in age, and...

'I must be off,' said James. 'Don't any of you work too hard.'

Jane must just have him with her for a few moments longer. 'I'll just walk with you to the lift.' The smile she spared for her colleague held some of the provocation usually reserved for her husband. 'And you *will* wait, Arthur, won't you? I have things... I'll be back in a minute.'

Pleased that her ploy to detain him for a little longer had succeeded, still more pleased that the staff landing, which could be busy at that time of day, was deserted, she touched her fingers to his. 'James...' Her voice was all breathy, inviting as the mouth held up to his. But she encountered a raised eyebrow, a cynical glint, and, instead of a kiss, he was mocking the appeal she had made just a moment before.

'"You *will* wait, Arthur?"' It was a fair shot at the tone she had accidentally used. '"There are things... things I want to tell you. I'll be back in a moment, Arthur".' His finger stabbed impatiently at the button.

'James?' For a moment she was bewildered, then she gave a little laugh. 'James!' Now she was frowning, mildly disapproving as she put a hand up to his cheek.

'Don't mind me.' His grin, his shrug were slightly apologetic.

'You're not still jealous?' She ought to have been angry, indignant, but she wasn't. Rather...flattered.

'I am—I admit it. Jealous.' The lift reached their floor, the doors slid open and she was pulled inside, held by powerful hands on her shoulders. 'Jealous of anyone who's known you a day longer than I have.' The doors closed with a soft clunk.

'James!' Impossible to know whether to laugh or to protest, but her work...Arthur... 'James,' she used her wide green eyes to some effect, gazing up at him, 'I must get back to the office. They'll all wonder...'

'Let them.'

'Someone might come in.' His arms folded about her.

'I don't mind.'

'But I do... I must... Oh, James!' His mouth was intent on smothering her protest.

'I'll let you out,' at last the possessiveness of his arms relaxed and she could breathe again, 'on one condition only.'

'Oh, James,' she was confused, but also she was excited, 'I must go.' There was a lipstick smear on his mouth. She dabbed at it with her handkerchief, then tried to repair the damage to her own appearance. 'What do you mean?'

'Remember earlier? When I suggested you stay at home for another day?' She nodded, not quite seeing what he was leading up to. 'And you behaved with extreme provocation?'

'Did I?' She coloured guiltily, tried to avoid his eyes and even glanced at the closed lift doors as if they might be in danger of performing for the entertainment of the entire staff of the magazine.

'You know exactly what I mean.'

'Please, please let me out!' She reached for the floor button, but he caught her hand in time.

'When you promise.'

'You haven't told me what...'

'I want the performance repeated.' She stared up, recognising the mischievous glint but still not understanding. 'In reverse,' he added, then laughed softly as her green eyes widened. 'I see you've caught my drift. And you needn't look so scandalised.'

'I'm going.' This time he didn't try to stop her pressing the button, and the doors began to open.

'You promise?'

'Yes, I promise.' She was breathless, confused, still a little shy, unaccustomed as yet to some of the more delectable aspects of marriage. Safely in the corridor, she turned round.

'Remember,' James raised a finger as the doors closed for the last time, 'I shall hold you to it. Tonight.'

When Jane got back to the office she knew she was still blushing madly, afraid to glance at Arthur and grateful when Lottie, ever dependable, produced a pot of coffee and cups.

'Well, now,' Arthur stirred for a moment or two before sipping and putting down the cup on the corner of the desk, 'I must say the married state suits you, Jane. You look blooming.'

Very conscious of exactly what had put that bloom of happiness on her cheeks, Jane turned away, apparently in search of some papers in the filing cabinet. 'Well, you know, so much sun, sea and...' Again she was grateful when Lottie pushed over the photographs.

'Some lovely snaps, Mr Davis.' Lottie rolled a piece of paper into her machine, squinting down at her notes. 'I'm sure you'd like to have a look at them,' and she began to type.

'Mmm, most attractive.' Arthur merely glanced at them before pushing aside his cup and getting to his feet. 'I wanted to warn you, Jane, there's a heads of department meeting scheduled for Thursday, and as you're in charge while Mrs Devere is on sick leave the management will expect you to be there. I thought I'd better just warn you, though there'll be a notice coming round. About two-thirty, I think it is.' He smiled at her again. 'Nice to see you back again, Jane—I've missed you.' The door closed behind him.

There was a moment's silence before Lottie spoke. 'Poor Mr Davis.'

'Why do you say that, Lottie?' Jane was anxious to have her own suspicions denied. 'Poor isn't an adjective I'd apply to Arthur.'

'No—silly of me. But he's always had such a soft spot for you—you know that without me telling you. Ever since you started here as an eighteen-year-old trainee.'

'Yes,' Jane gave a weary sigh, 'I suppose I do know. But there's never been anything... A visit to a show once or twice a year, nothing more than that.'

'Yes, I know. But I expect they were the highlights of his existence.'

'I do hope they weren't, Lottie,' Jane felt indefinably uneasy, 'otherwise he must lead a pretty dreary existence.'

'But he does, love. Didn't you tell me about his awful old mother?'

'Oh, dear!' Jane showed a touch of guilt. 'Did I say awful? I suppose I must have. Certainly she has Arthur completely under her thumb and she was most suspicious of me. I wonder if she really believed I had designs on him?'

'Well, I don't think he's the marrying kind.'

'And if he were, there'd be no likelihood of him marrying me, and...'

'And talking of mothers, Jane, tell me, how did your parents react when you rang and said you were getting married?'

'Total and complete panic is the answer to that— just about what you'd expect. James wasn't too far out when he said they flew out determined to stop the wedding, but then...' In the act of extracting one particular file from the cabinet, Jane paused, gazing dreamily out of the window.

'But then,' laughter gurgled in Lottie's throat, 'then they met James. And that was the end of all opposition.'

'Well, not quite.' Jane closed the drawer decisively. 'They did their best to persuade us to postpone, but when they saw how things were...in the end I think they realised it *was* hopeless, and they gave in quite gracefully.'

'Fell under the James Barnard spell, is that what you mean? Rather as I did.'

'Just that. Do you know, Lottie, I can't remember what life was like before I met James—is that difficult to believe?'

'Not really. I think most of us feel like that at the beginning.' Lottie sighed as she rolled another sheet of paper into her machine. 'The problem is keeping it up.'

But Jane wasn't listening. She was concentrating on the details, descriptions and price lists on the papers in front of her. And wondering with a desperate aching emptiness just how she was going to exist without James for what was very nearly...a whole *day*. And after that...

She shivered.

CHAPTER THREE

SATURDAY evening crowds were ghastly, but even
the dreary journey home couldn't damp down
Jane's elation. She discovered by the simple means
of a glimpse in a dark reflecting window that she
was sitting there smiling to herself as she huddled
in the corner of the crowded train. An embarrassed
upward glance confirmed that the strap-hanging
male was responding in a very positive way, so it
was a relief to feel the train slowing as it approached her station. She got to her feet with as
much self-possession as she could muster, her
newspaper folded firmly under her arm.

'I just can't remember where we met.' His well-
modulated voice was low in an attempt at intimacy.

'I'm sure we haven't.' She moved to grasp the
upright pole, making sure that her ringed left hand
was clearly in evidence.

'Pity!' Both smile and shrug were regretful, but
at least he made no attempt to delay her or to follow
her from the train. He was probably well versed in
both the approach and brush-off—or encouragement—and accepted both philosophically.

Moments later Jane was walking briskly along
their quiet road, pulling her dark coat more closely
about her to exclude the chilly wind. It was a

nuisance that Tenterden House was so much further from the station than her old flat. From that point of view it was less convenient, but there was compensation, of course. James's flat was so much more spacious, certainly more luxurious and.... She reached the wide plate-glass doors, waving to the porter, who was emerging from his cubicle just as she pressed the lift button.

Sounds of music from the sitting-room took her straight in there. James was on the couch, his back to her. She paused for a moment, tenderness flooding her as she absorbed pure pleasure from the scene. *Home.* It had been that since their first day back. And it was nothing to do with the soft lighting, the elegant modern furniture, but everything to do with him, the man she had married. James and home were synonymous. Where he was, there was home.

A few steps, and she leaned over, putting her cheek against his, knowing he would be enveloped in a wave of delicate perfume. She had used the spray for his benefit just before leaving the office. 'Hi!' Her excitement rose again as she tried to judge his reaction at her news. 'Have you had a nice day? Have you missed me?'

'I always miss you.' Though he didn't turn there was a smile in his voice and his hand came up to circle the nape of her neck, a finger stroking idly. 'Especially when you're not here. Come closer,' he patted the seat beside him, 'so I can show you exactly how much I've missed you.'

'Just a moment.' Jane slipped out of her jacket, kicked off her shoes and went round to lie back on the settee, her head resting on his knees, one hand extended to touch his cheek. 'It's so good to be home, you wouldn't believe.' She closed her eyes, wriggled into a more comfortable position and moaned from sheer pleasure.

He smiled down at her, pursed his lips, then frowned. 'Has it ever occurred to you that if it wasn't for Beaumont's we could have whole weekends at home together instead of——?'

Her eyes shot open as she heard the name of her company. All afternoon she had been simmering with her news; now she was bubbling, and she hadn't even noticed his implied criticism. 'Oh—and speaking of the firm, I've just heard the most wonderful thing...' she began.

'Now let me guess.' He appeared to consider. 'I know—you've at last managed to get rid of that bearskin coat that's been cluttering up the props wardrobe since 1928!'

'Wrong.' She extricated herself and sat up, beginning to undo her jade earrings. 'Besides, you know we stopped promoting fur coats years ago. But try again.' By now she was unfastening the buttons of her blouse, pulling it from the waist of her skirt.

James stood for a moment watching her with the expression which made her blood quicken, grinning as he reached out his fingers and slid them across the smooth skin of her shoulders. 'Not fair,' he stated lazily, then, as he felt her shudder, 'My feelings exactly.' His voice was low as if there were danger from eavesdroppers. 'You're being very provoking—you know that, don't you, asking a question, then setting out quite deliberately to distract? But let me see . . .' He folded her against him, his hands slipping down below her waist and pressing her close. 'News from Beaumont's—I've got it. They've found a huge discrepancy in the books and the Fraud Squad are grilling the chief accountant.'

'You. . .' Jane looked up, teeth slightly bared, then dropped a tiny biting kiss on his chin. 'You are disgusting, James Barnard. What has poor Arthur Davis ever done to you?'

'That——' she knew they were joking, teasing, but there was a sharp little edge to his voice telling her he still had some reserves '—that, my sweet, is just what I'd like to know.'

'Anyway, you're wrong again—it's not that. Besides, didn't I tell you that Arthur is a very wealthy man in his own right? At least he will be one day. His mother owns property all over London.'

'I'm not going to talk about Arthur. He's way down my list right at this moment.'

'You brought him up, didn't you?' She gave a little scream and caught at his fingers. 'Anyway, I'm going to have a shower, so you needn't waste any time on *that*.'

'No? Is that a challenge, by any chance?'

'Absolutely not.' She was smiling, eyes brilliant, breath quickened.

'And yet I remember a time...not so very long ago. Aha, you can still blush, I see.'

'For that,' she whirled away, tossing her blouse back towards him, stalking through the bedroom, casting clothes in all directions as she went, 'for that I shall make you wait! You can die of curiosity before... In any case——' She reached for her shower cap, stepped into the cubicle and into the warm jet. 'In any case,' when she emerged he was still lounging on the chair watching her. He reached out for a fleecy warm towel, threw it about her shoulders and crossed it gently in front while she was unpinning her hair, raking it with long pink-tipped fingers, 'I promised myself on the way home that we'd go out for a meal. A celebration. I'll tell you my news over a glass of champagne.'

'A celebration, is it?' His eyes widened, and if his glance skimmed over her figure with an expression of intense speculation she didn't notice.

'I know you'll be pleased for me,' she added.

'Oh?' There was no mistaking the flatness of his tone as he turned away.

'James,' by now she was sitting at her dressing-table brushing her hair, the towel fixed sarong-style under her arms, 'is anything the matter?'

'Nothing.' He shrugged. 'Nothing's the matter except...going out for a meal. There really isn't anything so very special about it. We're out pretty often, after all.'

'But,' skilfully Jane smeared cream over her face and neck, 'I don't mean the pub on the corner—that's just to save cooking, after all.' Although she was a little disconcerted by his attitude she must try not to show it. 'I was rather thinking of that little bistro—do you remember, when we were coming back from that visit to the parents we saw it and promised ourselves a meal there some time? Can you remember what it was called?'

'Le Lapin Blanc. Or it might have been brown, that one. Not too far from the Barbican, I seem to recall.'

'I thought we might go there.' Then, to dispel what she imagined was the beginning of a frown, 'My treat.'

'Oh, well, so long as you're paying.' James went out of the room, and Jane stared after him in bewilderment. Sarcasm was something she hadn't encountered from him but that was undoubtedly what it was, and for a moment she was downcast. This evening had been meant to be special, but she was doing it all wrong. She ought to have told him at once about her promotion and they could have shared the decision about how to celebrate. He might have had some other ideas—after all, it was true enough, there was nothing very special about going out for a meal, and how naïve of her to offer to take care of the bill! That kind of thing you said to a girlfriend, not a husband. Especially not this particular husband, she thought with a little smile of complacency. James liked those things to be under his control—it was always *his* credit card...

Anyway, what the dickens, she didn't in the least mind if they went out or stayed in. In many ways the latter meant less effort. She could ring for a pizza, and there was some sparkling wine left over from the party they had had soon after they returned from Jamaica—that would be celebration enough for her.

Singing softly now, she began to dress, choosing a long skirt, one James had bought for her when they were on honeymoon, swirls of brilliant green on a dark ground, and a white blouse in crisp cotton with wide bracelet sleeves. Light make-up, hair brushed so it floated about her shoulders, then held back with a broad band. Another discreet blast of scent and she drifted through to the sitting-room.

James was leaning against the fireplace, supported by one elbow, fingers rubbing reflectively against his chin. The mirror on the wall behind him reflected the back of his head, and she was aware of her own figure standing for a moment in the doorway, then slowly walking towards him. They watched each other carefully, Jane taking in details which had only half registered before. Long legs in narrow finely checked trousers were crossed at the ankle, highly polished slip-on shoes, grey snakeskin belt resting low on his hip-bones, navy shirt, tie swirling with grey and coral.

'You're quite right.' Reaching him, she linked her arms confidently about his neck, offering her lips in a brushing, teasing contact, feeling a burst of triumph when she saw the gold-flecked eyes darken to a warm languorous brown. 'It's so much nicer to stay at home.'

'You know,' his arm tightened about her waist, 'you walk with the most provocative swagger. Coming or going, it makes no difference... It's about the first thing I noticed about you.'

'Mmm,' her eyelids drooped, forming tiny black fans against her cheeks, 'I thought the first thing you noticed about me was gin and tonic.'

'No,' his breath was hurrying, 'even before that... I saw you in that short suede skirt. And I made up my mind right then...' He nibbled gently at her ear.

'Yes, what?' She felt heady, wonderfully relaxed.

'I thought... well, I don't think I'd better tell you what I thought.'

'*James*!'

'I thought you were quite the most fascinating woman I'd ever seen, and...' he held her at arm's length, laughing down into her surprised expression '... and have you any idea how hungry I am?'

'So that's why you married me, is it?' With a look of mock reproof she walked away from him into the kitchen. 'To cook for you!'

'Among other things.' He stood watching as she tied an apron about her waist and began opening cupboards. 'Cooking wasn't exactly in the forefront of my mind at the time.'

'No?' Taking a bowl of whipped cream from the fridge, Jane took a blob on her finger and transferred it to her mouth. 'Maybe just as well. I wouldn't list it at the top of my accomplishments. But I am pretty good at salads.' She dangled some plastic bags of greenery in front of his eyes before turning to reach for a colander.

'Your mother's a good cook, and most women turn out like their mothers in the end,' James remarked.

'I just hope you don't starve while you're waiting.'

'Am I being unreasonable?' He reached out for a fat radish, and she heard him crunch as she washed the lettuce under the tap. 'Chaining you to the stove like this,' she turned round, raised a sardonic eyebrow before returning to what she was doing, 'when you would have preferred to eat out.'

'I didn't say I would have preferred it.' Emptying the contents of the colander into a salad drier, she quickly dried her hands. 'You can give that a couple of whirls while I make the dressing. No, I'd just as soon they stay at home, I just thought you deserved to eat well, that's all, but we can celebrate just as well at home.'

'Ah, yes, the celebration.' James's tone was thoughtful. 'It looks as if you had an exciting day, and so in a way did I. I have some rather special news too, something that deserves a decent wine . . . I'd better go and open the bottle.'

*   *   *

'Come on, then.' They had enjoyed the meal in spite of its simplicity, and when he leaned forward, smiling at her over the pink candles as he topped up her glass, Jane new the moment had come. 'Tell all,' he ordered. 'I'm dying with curiosity!'

'Well,' she had been hugging the news to her since lunchtime, sharing it with no one, intense in her determination that he should be the first to know, 'you know, don't you, that Mrs Devere has been off work for the last four, nearly five months?'

'Mmm, she damaged her spine slipping on some ice—yes, you told me that.'

'Well, she's finally decided she won't be coming back, so...' Jane's green eyes widened, gleaming with excitement ' ... I was summoned at lunchtime today, introduced to the chairman of the company no less, and was formally offered the job.'

'So...' His eyes had narrowed slightly, lips pursed, and he was maybe a little less impressed than she would have liked. 'And now I suppose they've given you some time to consider the offer?'

'Consider?' Unable to sit still any longer, she jumped up, knocked her glass, caught it just in time, then invited herself to sit on his knee, her arms linked round his neck. 'What was there to consider? Didn't I tell you, I've been waiting for that job for the past five years? Oh, not that I'm not sad about Mrs Devere...'

'Naturally.' Drily and with that underlying hint of sarcasm which she was too elated to notice.

'But I said yes at once. I know I can do the job, maybe even better than Mrs Devere—she was getting into a rut, and—oh, James, there'll be such opportunities! I'll be doing all the fashion shows in Paris and Rome and...oh,' she faltered, conscious that maybe she had come to his reasons for reservation; it would undoubtedly mean a tighter schedule and he already thought her hours were long enough, 'I know it won't be much fun when I'm away,' his face was impassive now, giving no clue to his real feelings, 'but of course I'll be earning much more money.'

That, she realised too late, was something she should have avoided. 'More for the taxman' would be his reaction, but she hurried on, 'You know, of course, that I'll be on a much higher salary as an editor, so it does make a difference.' Her voice faded and with it a little of her confidence. It wasn't turning out as she had imagined, which was a pity. If he had had some unexpected promotion she would be delighted for him. She pressed on, determined to take no notice. 'You know what Sir Jocelyn said—"We'll have to be careful of our Mrs Barnard, we'll be in danger of seeing her headhunted by our rivals." *Our* Mrs Barnard!' Again her voice trailed away. 'James,' there was a pleading tone, 'please say you're happy for me!'

It was a second before he answered, and though his smile was still rather strained that fact did not register until later. 'I'm happy for you, Jane. Delighted—of course I am. And very proud. And

I agree with Sir Jocelyn, half the magazines in London will be out to steal you from under his nose. Only...'

'James!' Partly reassured, Jane smiled up at him, but her eyes as they searched his face were anxious. 'As if I'd ever leave Beaumont's! Not a word to them about that, of course. The board knows I've had my sights set on the job for years, I've always told you that, and——'

'Yes. Yes, my darling, you always did tell me that.' Now his eyes were so shadowed, so troubled, that it was impossible to quash her rapidly rising apprehension.

'James?' A tentative query in her voice as she remembered he had news. She was about to ask him to explain when he sighed deeply and spoke again.

'Yes, Jane,' his voice was lacking its normal upbeat tone, 'since we first met you've made no secret of having your sights firmly fixed on that job. And that's what makes me so reluctant to spoil things for you. You must know I'd do anything in the world to avoid doing that, but——'

'James!' Another minute and she would scream with frustration. She took one or two deep calming breaths. 'As if anything you ever did would spoil things for me.' But she couldn't ignore this sinking feeling in the pit of her stomach; she even had a wild urge to clamp her hands over her ears, to escape from whatever was threatening them, to make for the security of a darkened bedroom.

Was it all to do with money? It was a subject James had always been slightly touchy about, old-fashioned in a way, though he was ahead of the group in almost every other aspect of life. She had been wrong, hasty to make any mention of her increase in salary. On the other hand, everyone these days acknowledged that women were every bit as entitled to interesting, well paid jobs as men. It wasn't as if he had any need to feel insecure; they each had exactly what they wanted both in the workplace and domestically, absolutely, and . . .

'I'm so desperately sorry, darling.' He got to his feet, one hand reaching out to touch hers in a conciliatory gesture. Then he raked his fingers through his hair with an air of distraction little short of desperate. 'You see, I've been on the telephone most of the day—you know our parent company has its headquarters in Houston, and there've been some pretty far-reaching changes taking place. The long and the short of it is, Jane, we're leaving London very shortly. I've got a new appointment in Brazil and we'll be going there to live.'

There was an endless silence. Jane felt as if she had suffered an enormous blow to her heart and for the moment was unable to say a word. Eyes desperately searching his for a sign that she had misunderstood, she stood there looking. But maybe he had been joking. He must have been teasing, suggesting that if she had been offered a new job then so had he. It must be that. Her spirits soared accordingly. And crashed when the expression on his face, concerned, anxious, got through to her.

But how could it be? Things like this just didn't happen. Minutes before, or so it seemed, she had been the woman with everything in the world going for her, married to this man who just took her breath away, and now... the certainty of reaching the summit in her chosen career and why... she couldn't understand why it should all change to ashes.

At last, making a superhuman effort, she forced her lips to move. 'Wh-what did you say, James?' A tiny grimace. 'For a moment I thought...'

'Darling,' she resented the faint note of pleading in his voice, 'you'll love it when we get there...'

So it was true, then. She felt quite distinctly all the colour drain from her face, her legs grew weak and rubbery, so when her hand encountered the back of a chair she sank into it with a feeling of relief.

Brazil, she thought he had said, but she must have got it wrong. Then the word echoed again in her mind and she knew with dreadful certainty that there was no mistake. And she knew, also with dreadful certainty, that whoever might be going to Brazil to live, she, Jane Barnard, would be staying in London, and that meant... she wasn't prepared to allow James to leave. It was as simple as that.

CHAPTER FOUR

'JAMES——' In a comparatively short time Jane had become quite adept at getting her own way. In fact he was so indulgent that it was hard for her to visualise a situation where her wheedling wouldn't work. Especially if she came up behind him as she did now, wrapping her arms about him, leaning her cheek against his shoulderblade like this. He would respond in one of several ways, but each one leading with delicious inevitability towards the bedroom door. 'James, we are going to talk about it, aren't we?'

But now she felt him stiffen, not the reaction she looked or hoped for. Instead of turning round to cradle her in his arms he took a step forward, rather pointedly away from her, picking up the papers he had been involved with when she arrived back from work.

'Of course.' He flicked a glance at her, but without appearing to notice she was wearing the green silk blouse he particularly liked— 'Exactly the colour of your eyes, my darling,' —and returned his attention almost at once to his fascinating business correspondence. 'What is it you want to discuss?'

She felt the draught as if a door had been deliberately slammed in her face, the sting of tears behind her eyes, but they were washed away by the following and wholly unexpected wave of anger. How dared he do this to her, how could he be so callous, causing her so much anxiety? Especially right now when he was well aware of her position, when she was so involved in reorganising the department, when he knew how important it was for her to get on top of her job. She would never have believed he would be so inconsiderate ... When she replied her voice told much of what she felt; it was so much more brisk than usual, the one she used when dealing with a careless junior.

'I'd have thought that was perfectly obvious.' And to underline her exasperation she strode into the kitchen, high heels tapping angrily on the tiled floor, pretending to be busy at the sink. It was a moment before James followed—an additional annoyance, this, but she was well aware of the precise instant when he came to stand in the doorway watching her through narrowed eyes. It pleased her to ignore him for a second or two, giving no sign until she turned round. He was directly in her vision while she dried her hands. 'Well, isn't it?' she challenged abrasively.

'You mean about us going to Brazil?' The mild tone seemed calculated to irritate still further, but she was learning to count to ten, and she did it right then—slowly, staring at him as she shook out the towel and returned it to its hook. How was it she had never realised that men could be so...difficult was an understatement...provoking, deliberately awkward and...?

'About the job *you* have been offered.' She nodded. 'Yes, I certainly think it's a matter we ought to discuss. Don't you?'

'Mmm.' Agreement, perhaps. But if so certainly half-hearted. 'Only,' he was still frowning over his papers as if they were of far more interest than the matter she had brought up, 'I decided it best to let the matter settle down for a few days longer. You were so opposed to the idea in the first pl——'

'And I still am.'

'But I knew when you reconsidered you'd see all the plus points. It's a fascinating country, Jane, you'd love it, and we could have a wonderful life...'

'I love my own country. I find it fascinating.' Her tone was passionate, and again she felt the unaccustomed sting of tears. 'I love my job, our life here in this flat—it's all I ever dreamed of having.'

'And you've always loved travel. Since we met you've been telling me how much you envied me and wished you'd had half my opportunities.'

'I always loved going away on holiday,' she wailed, thinking with regret of those nights when she curled up beside him on the settee, encouraging him to tell stories about remote and fascinating countries. The last thing she had imagined was having them quoted back at her... '*And* coming back home again. I've never said, not once, that I wanted to live abroad.'

'Look, darling——' It was so obvious he was making a superhuman effort to be reasonable, and that in itself was irritating, as if she were a difficult child who had to be coaxed from her ill humour. He came towards her then, reached out a hand to brush her cheek with the back of his fingers. His expression was gentle and he was looking his usual devastating self. The tall rangy figure suited casual clothes as well as the more formal ones, blue and white checked shirt topped by blue cashmere pullover, navy cords. He never looked less than dangerously attractive, and for the moment Jane felt slightly resentful of that fact. 'Let's try to be rational about this—it's important to us both, after all. I've been ordered to Brazil for the next two years and I want... I *expect* you to come with me. That's all there is to it.'

'No!' Anger, frustration, the desire to hit back, to knock him out of his cocoon of complacency, made her tremble. She wrapped her arms about herself to hide the shaking that could so easily have been identified as weakness, turning away so her decision had no chance of being affected by any appeal she saw in his eyes. 'No,' she spoke more moderately, 'unfortunately that's *not* all there is to it. There's a great deal more to be taken——'

'Would you rather I *didn't* care? That's how it's beginning to look, if I didn't mind if you came or not? Tell me, what would you think if that was the situation, would you be happier then?'

'What I would rather...is for you to realise that you aren't the only one with a career. In fact,' she struggled with thoughts that had been bugging her since first he had dropped his bombshell, thoughts which discretion had dictated she keep to herself but which now were irresistible, 'in fact, it isn't so long since you told me you weren't particularly ambitious.' She swung round, her hands extended palms upward in appeal. 'In that case, why don't you explain to the company, tell them you'd rather stay in London? Obviously they think highly of you or you wouldn't have been offered the job in Brazil, and that way, I'm sure they'd agree, we'd both have what we want.'

It was a long time before he spoke. He simply stood there looking at her, apparently oblivious of her eyes, wide and appealing, certainly unmoved by the rapid rise and fall of her breast beneath the silk blouse. At last he sighed, his shoulders moving in a faint dismissive shrug. 'No, Jane, what you mean is that in your scenario *you* would have what *you* want.'

'But you said...'

'I don't care what I said. If I said I wasn't ambitious that didn't mean I was prepared to toss away any opportunity that came my way. Don't you realise?' He frowned, strode across the room and back. 'Have you any idea what this job is? It's a *coup*, and I'd have to be a complete wimp to turn it down. Everyone would think I'd taken leave of my senses, and it would be the end of the line as far as Atlantic Oil is concerned. When I said I wasn't ambitious, what I probably meant was that I didn't put promotion at the top of my list of priorities—there are other things I value more. And one of them, strangely enough,' his fine eyes flashed now, telling her if she had been ignorant before that his anger could be a very potent force, 'is our marriage. And that's why I expect you to come to Brazil.'

'And maybe that's,' tears were stinging insistently now; she had to blink fiercely, to press her fingernails into the palms of her hand and even then she had difficulty in keeping her voice steady, 'that's why I find your determination to go so difficult to understand.' She left the room, hurriedly going into their bedroom, struggling for a few minutes to regain her control. Pleased, she assured herself as she blew her nose, glaring at her red-eyed reflection in the mirror, pleased and relieved that James hadn't followed her to witness her reaction.

A tiny smear of lipstick, a flick of powder would help raise her morale, but still—she adjusted the wide belt at her waist—they must try to resolve the situation, especially before their trip down to Sussex next weekend. There was no way she wanted her parents to suspect a problem in her marriage, not when they had flown out to the Caribbean to try to urge caution and had succumbed so totally when they met the man their daughter had fallen in love with. And in any case, there was no problem. At least, not one she was incapable of resolving. She sighed, sprayed herself with a little perfume and turned for the door.

'Look, Jane——' If she had expected the short break to effect any sort of capitulation she was mistaken. Now James was no longer troubling to hide his exasperation. He had poured himself a glass of whisky and soda, raised his glass in enquiry, accepted her firm shake of the head without comment. 'There's no use pretending, even if we are at the end of the twentieth century. A man's career is for life. That doesn't as a rule apply to young married women. Ask Lottie, if you want confirmation of that.'

'Oh, Lottie!' Her lip trembled betrayingly.

'Yes, Lottie. Lottie, whom you think so much of, whose opinion you respect so mightily. What did she say? Presuming, that is, you did discuss the matter with her.' He paused, and when she made no attempt to answer him, instead sighing loudly and making some fiddly unnecessary adjustments to the curtains, he persisted, 'Well, did you or did you not mention to Lottie that we were going to Brazil?'

'As a matter of fact, I did just mention that you'd been offered a job in Brazil,' Jane admitted.

'And . . .'

'And if you *must* know,' resenting the pressure and unwilling just then to admit just how enthusiastic Lottie's reaction to the news had been, she flared out, 'Lottie's opinion was that it might be an interesting experience.' Chinese water torture wouldn't have made her reveal just then what Lottie's exact words had been: 'You've got it made, Jane, haven't you? A wonderful trip to an exciting country—and with a man like your James in tow. I'm madly jealous!'

'But, Lottie, don't you see . . . ?' Experiencing something like despair that reliable supportive Lottie, the woman whom she could depend on through thick and thin, seemed unwilling to confirm her in her decision, Jane had heard her voice rise a degree or two. 'There's my job here. I can't throw it up, not now, just when I've reached the top—if you only knew how long I've waited for it! It's been my ambition ever since I came to Beaumont's to get the job of chief fashion editor when Maggie Devere retired.'

'What's a job?' Unimpressed, Lottie had rolled another sheet of paper into her machine. 'What's a job compared with husband and kids . . . there's just no contest, is there?' And of course from Lottie's point of view that was undoubtedly true. She made no secret of the fact that she worked solely to help put her twin sons through university and——

'I would have thought,' James interrupted her unsatisfactory recollections, and his comment was so apposite that it was as though he had a private line to her brain, 'I'd have thought most women when they married realised there would be circumstances when they'd want to take a break . . .'

But Jane was in no mood to give any quarter. She refused even to glance in the direction he was indicating and shook her head decisively. 'I never did. I promise you that it never crossed——'

'You never thought!' This was the man as she had first known him, James Barnard at his most beguiling and mesmeric, if she allowed him... Yielding would be so easy, such delight after all the torment of recent days, and... As if sensing her insecurity, he grasped both her elbows, holding her away from him, those warm glinting eyes holding hers with possessive confidence. 'You never thought...' His voice deepened, and a throb started in the pit of her stomach. The long dark column of his throat was right in front of her eyes, inviting her to reach up, to stroke the silky skin. Now his hands moved, linking behind her waist so she could lean back against them, looking up into his face, all her emotions laid bare for him. 'You never thought, my love, that one day,' a moment more and she would surrender, be persuaded to do anything he wanted, her own dreams and ambitions consigned to the dustbin, 'one day, in the not too distant future, we might want,' his eyes narrowed, his gaze became more searching as he willed her to conform, 'to have a baby?'

It was a moment before that last suggestion penetrated Jane's mind. She had been so obsessed, so mesmerised by his insidious persuasion that all logic was driven from her mind, but when it did register the spell was abruptly broken and she stepped back before he could do any more damage.

'No, James.' It was painful to break the link, painful to deny him when all she wanted was to make him happy, to be happy herself—how painful to see the mellow searching look turn cool and distant. 'I can honestly say I've scarcely ever thought of it. Maybe I'm not the maternal type.' And yet . . . a voice at the back of her mind was trying to insist, when James had mentioned it, when he had suggested that they might at some time decide to have a baby, there had been a response, a flicker of interest at least, and . . . that was all she was prepared to admit even in the dark privacy of her mind. 'My career has always meant everything to me. And,' she was prepared to be placatory as far as she could, 'since I met you, James, since we married, I have everything in the world I want. Here,' she emphasised in case there should be any misunderstanding. 'Right here in this flat.'

'You surprise me.' His voice was flat as he turned away from her. 'And I'm disappointed. I'd always assumed . . . But no matter.' He left the room and came back a moment or two later, shrugging himself into a navy and maroon jacket. 'I've got to go out and post this letter—oh, don't worry if I'm not back immediately . . .'

'Wh . . .' Jane felt a quite unreasonable shaft of fear. 'What do you mean?'

'I feel in need of some fresh air.' His smile was taut and perfunctory. 'I might just jog round the park once or twice if the rain holds off. I don't suppose ... you don't feel like joining me?'

'I've—I've got that article to finish for to-morrow.' She too gave a half-hearted smile. 'Any other time ...'

'Ah, yes, of course,' this time his smile was more openly sardonic, 'the article—I forgot.' He leaned forward so their cheeks just touched for a moment, then he stood looking down. 'Don't worry, I'm sure we'll work something out. Only it does make you think about the old saying, don't you think?' He turned and stood with his fingers on the doorknob. 'When you marry as impetuously as we did you hardly have time to get to know each other properly. Shan't be long.'

And she was left gazing at the closed door, all kinds of negative words echoing in her ears, and the most insistent was disappointment. He was disappointed, with her, and she could not bear it.

And yet she must. If she were to give in now she would have to abandon every plan she had ever had, and truly—she used the caveat as some kind of justification—marriage had never been one of her long-term aims, it had simply happened. Not that she regretted it, rather she rejoiced in the fact that she and James had met, had 'recognised' each other almost immediately, and there was nothing about it that she would alter if she could.

Except this one thing. She must persuade James to give up thoughts of going abroad to live. There would be other opportunities for him later on, and she might at some time in the future feel she had proved herself in her career. She would feel more relaxed about it, might even be prepared to have a shot at something else.

But as for that other suggestion—she couldn't really imagine it, maybe because she had never thought of it, but if it was so important to James... She sighed wearily and moved to pick up the sheaf of papers and photographs which were to form the basis of a feature ironically called 'Winter Brides'. There had been simply no time to deal with this at work, but she had never felt less inclined to give an article the attention it demanded.

Disappointed. No matter how she tried to ignore the word it was determined to etch itself on her heart, painfully, like burning with acid. Tears filled her eyes so the pictures and words on the papers blurred and merged as she tried to regain control, but it was a few moments before she felt able to release her lower lip and to throw away her tissues. She must not let that happen again. A trickle could in no time become a cataract, and where would that leave *Beaumonde*'s important feature article? Her private life must not be allowed to impinge on the professional. She sat down at her desk and strove to concentrate.

CHAPTER FIVE

'I THINK, Nancy——' James had waited till they finished dinner and were about to move into the sitting-room for coffee before sending Jane a warning glance across the table, then he turned his head, smiling at her mother in that lazy way irresistible to women of all ages. And her mother was responding exactly as she would have expected, in the way she herself would be reacting in twenty years' time. Except—a stab of pain and something very much like fear stabbed at her midriff—except... She tried to smile at both her parents as James continued, 'Your daughter has some news for you.'

'Really, Jane?' Nancy Wyatt, who was in the act of picking up an ashtray, paused thoughtfully before pushing it along the cloth where it might catch some of her husband's cigar ash. She glanced speculatively towards her daughter. There was an air of excited anticipation which she was doing her best to keep under control, and a faint colour touched her cheeks. 'Then do tell us.' As she sat she exchanged a look with her husband, knowing and verging on the complacent. 'Don't keep us in suspense, darling!'

And that single glance practically submerged her daughter in a wave of embarrassment and irritation. It was so very obvious how their minds were working. And it suited her to put that down to James. If he had been more straightforward, less mysterious . . .

'Yes,' she hurried on, anxious now to put the record straight before things could get out of control. 'You know Mrs Devere's been on the sick list for ages—well, at last,' the look she sent her husband was deliberately challenging, 'she's decided to give up, and naturally,' disturbed by something about the way James was watching her so closely, she looked quickly away, wrinkling her nose self-deprecatingly towards her father, 'naturally, they offered me the job.'

'Darling!' There was a brief silence before the congratulations started, a silence that left Jane in no doubt that her parents had hoped to hear something quite different. 'That's wonderful news! Isn't it, Alan?' Nancy appealed to Jane's father. 'We both know how much you wanted that job.'

Now when Jane looked at her husband, an eyebrow raised as she invited him to take note of what her mother had just said, all she could see was the faint curl of his lips. Clearly he thought any job apart from his own wasn't worth . . .

'Yes, congratulations, Jane. You've worked hard there and I knew you'd make it. At least the board have had the sense to recognise who's been carrying the department for the last six months—

they'd have been crazy to look elsewhere. I think that maybe this calls for another drink—a toast. What will it be ... port, brandy?'

'But James has some news too,' Jane interrupted coolly, looking across the table at her husband. They had discussed at length how they were going to break things to her parents. First news of Jane's promotion would be broken, then his. She hoped that few questions would be asked, specific advice was the last thing she wanted, but at the same time she didn't want them to imagine ... 'Darling ...' With a little gesture she invited him to take the stage while she withdrew from the limelight. And she tried not to feel wounded by the blatant cynicism of his expression.

'But ...' When he had completed his brief an- nouncement there was a moment's silence before both parents spoke simultaneously and, it was im- possible not to take note of the fact, with all the enthusiasm which had been missing after Jane's news. 'That's *the* most wonderful surprise! I can't tell you how thrilled I am for you both!' Her mother was positively bubbling with delight.

'Yes, great news, James. You must be pleased, especially as you say it was so unexpected.'

'We shall miss you, naturally. It'll be quite a wrench not seeing you for such a long time, but ...' Nancy, with the addition of a glass of port to the wine she had taken at dinner, was noticeably skittish, almost flirting with her son-in-law. 'I've always longed to go to South America—I don't know why, maybe something I read about the High Andes——'

'I don't think the Andes are exactly in Brazil, Nancy.' Alan Wyatt shrugged his shoulders apologetically at the other two, but his wife brushed his interruption aside.

'Hush, darling! Can't you see, I'm trying to coax an invitation out of them? We'd love to go to Brazil on a visit, so if you'd be kind enough to ask us...'

For just a second no one spoke, but before the silence could become awkward James grinned, and only Jane realised how much of an effort he must have found it. She herself had been aware of mounting tension since she had got out of bed this morning, and now it was lodged, a great stone in the middle of her chest. She looked at him, her eyes aching with tears as she waited for him to deal with the question, not one they had covered beforehand. 'Of course you're both invited. You don't really have to ask, only...' Now his smile became obviously forced, the face he turned to their daughter visibly accusing. These are your parents, he was saying silently, and your actions are causing a lot of anxiety, but I'm the one who's having to talk us out of it. 'Only you'll have to be prepared to put up with my company, you see. Jane has decided to stay behind in London, she's had this wonderful opportunity with Beaumont's and...it's rather unfortunate that they've coincided. As you said, it's what she's always wanted, so it looks as if Jane won't be coming out to Brazil.'

No one spoke, but three pairs of eyes were all at once looking at Jane. She was the focus of so much critical amazement that she longed to put up her hands to push them back.

'But, Jane,' it was a relief when her mother spoke, even though her tone of disbelief said almost more than the words she used, 'you can't possibly mean that! You're not going to let James go off to Brazil on his own!'

'He's a grown man, Mother.' She chose to misinterpret her meaning. 'He's been around a lot, and I think he's quite capable of finding Brazil without me having to hold his hand while he does.'

'That, and you know it, Jane, is not what I meant.'

'It's a great opportunity, Jane.' Her father had always been more diplomatic than her mother. 'If you don't take it, you might spend the rest of your life regretting it.'

'It *is* a great opportunity, I know that.' She was fighting to retain her calm, but it was difficult to raise the glass without revealing exactly how shaken she was. She fixed her eyes on the dark wine, waited for a moment before sipping slowly once or twice. 'But you see,' carefully she replaced her drink on the table before looking at them—three faces, she told herself, each showing complete lack of understanding, even antagonism; it was very hard to bear, 'even before I knew about James's promotion I'd accepted the job at Beaumont's. It was Sir Jocelyn himself who said I'd been selected. I got the idea they'd all been waiting for Mrs Devere to make up her mind so they could give me the job. And I was thrilled—what else could you expect?—and I said yes straight away.' Right now Jane refused to look at her husband. He had no right to try to influence her. Words were one thing, you could always argue back, but such a blank expression, disapproving, was unfair, more difficult to deal with. It wasn't as if she didn't know all there was to know about his disappointment—surprising how the word stung...

'Oh, darling, is that all you're worrying about?' The relief in her mother's voice brought Jane from her reverie and her head up with a jerk. 'I don't think you should worry any more about it. Sir Jocelyn will understand when you explain about James. He won't try to keep you to your promise.'

'You haven't signed a contract, have you, Janey?' Her father, a businessman himself, raised what he thought was an important point.

'No, not yet, there hasn't been time. I——'

'There you are, then, there's nothing they can do about it, and——'

'*Mother*!' Jane felt her hard-won patience and self-control begin to slip away. 'Of course there's nothing they can do about it, but can't you understand? They've offered me a job, the job I set my heart on years ago, the one I've been working towards since I first joined the company. I want the job—I've always wanted it. What I do not want is to see someone else step into my shoes.'

'James!' Now Nancy Wyatt, having failed with her daughter, turned to her son-in-law in appeal. 'I just don't understand. Surely you're not prepared to allow your wife to act——?'

'Mother!' The tone was verging on outrage.

'There's no use speaking to me in that way, Jane. You should remember you're no longer on your own, you're a married woman now.'

'I had noticed that, as a matter of fact.'

'Nancy,' James spoke gently but with a degree of firmness that caused them both to turn, Jane in time to find herself at the receiving end of a look that was just short of searing, 'Jane knows exactly how I feel. She knows what I want her to do.'

'But,' Alan Wyatt was frowning, concerned and possibly, thought Jane miserably, her only ally here. He had always been the most indulgent of fathers, willing to be twisted round her little finger. 'James, you're not saying...surely you want Jane to be with you? You've been married just a few months, and...' He shrugged. 'It's so hard to understand.'

'Of course James wants me to go with him, Daddy!' Jane spoke sharply, determined there should be no misunderstanding on that score. 'But you must see... I still want to keep my own job. I love it, and——'

'You must *do* something, James! There must be some way you can persuade her——'

'I've told her how I feel, Nancy,' he interrupted with a trace of weariness. 'But Jane must in the end make up her own mind. I know how important her job is to her.' At least he was showing some loyalty, implying that her decision was the result of much rational discussion, attempts to reach a compromise, not letting them know how much passionate argument, how many attempts at persuasion had come to nothing.

'Then in that case, Jane, there's no reason for you to be so——'

'Please, Mother!' Her nerves were jangling, Jane was on the verge of breaking and no one even seemed to notice. These three people—tumultuously she looked round at them—the most important people in her world, and none seemed capable of looking at things from her point of view. Instead, accusation was writ large on each face. Oh, why had they decided to come down here this weekend? If she had been hoping for some degree of support from her own parents then she was in for a disappointment. It was hard to bear. All her life...she swallowed at the lump in her throat...for as long as she could remember they had been supportive, admiring each tiny step, each rung up the ladder, but now, when she needed them most... She controlled an impulse to shout and protest, but it was impossible to eliminate the accusation as she looked at her parents. 'And you, Father—I'm surprised at you both! How many times have I heard you supporting the woman's point of view, her right to be treated as an individual, but now, when it comes to the crunch any sense of balance has flown out of the window.' Warming to her theme, she became more passionate. 'I notice neither of you has even hinted that James might take a rain check on *his* career. It's simply taken for granted that any sacrifice is to be done by the woman. We might just as well be back in the Stone Age for all that's changed! Suppose,' her green eyes blazed at each of them in turn, 'just suppose I was a world-class scientist, what would you say then, would you still think my career didn't matter? I'm very much afraid you would. And now,' she pushed back her chair and got to her feet, 'it seems there's nothing much to say, so I think I'll have a bath and go to bed. I've had a trying week and I'm rather tired.' With careful precision she replaced her chair and left the room, closing the door behind her with masterly restraint.

It was quite some time before James joined his wife in the bedroom, and by that time she was delicately scented from the body cream she had applied after her bath, her hair was brushed about her shoulders and she had a book propped open against her knees. It had been opened at random and so far she had been unable to concentrate on a single word. She was too busy reliving the scene she had created down there in the dining-room. It was a bit embarrassing to find that at the age of twenty-seven she could still act like a teenager. Not that she regretted or withdrew a single word, only... maybe one day she would learn to get her own way by stealth and guile.

Which was one of the reasons she had brought this new nightdress with her. Even at discount price it had been hideously expensive, but if it achieved her object it would be money well spent. The peach satin was skilfully cut to flatter, the bodice inset with chiffon, trimmed with lace, slender straps of rolled silk, one of which slipped from her shoulder just as the door opened and James came into the room.

Her heart was hammering. She put up a hand to brush the hair back from her face, all the while observing his every move from the concealing fringe of lashes. He said nothing, just stood for a moment at the door, then began to walk about the large bedroom, pulling his shirt over his head, then, as always, having to struggle to undo his cufflinks—the times she had teased him about his habit. A tiny giggle helped relieve her tension as he stood in front of the mirror frowning over the fiddly task.

Then a gasp when she realised she in her turn was being scrutinised. He swung round, came towards the bed and picked up the pyjama trousers which were what he usually wore, totally unconscious, or so it seemed, of the effect he was having on her. 'That,' he said, his brown eyes cool and detached, 'was quite a performance down there.'

'Mmm.' Jane put aside the book, fascinated as she always was by the silky brown skin but determined to look down at her fingernails. 'I didn't mean it to be; it's how it happened.'

'You do know, I suppose,' he slid into the bed beside her, reaching behind to adjust the pillows, 'that you're wearing your necklace?'

'Am I?' Surprise had never been so well contrived. 'Oh,' she reached up to grasp the crystal which hung low on the silver chain, 'I forgot about it.' She got out of bed, walked to the dressing-table and began to fiddle with the catch. The reflection assured her she had his whole attention. He was watching with a strange, intent expression. She was also conscious that her pulse and breathing were more erratic. She whirled away from the glass and appealed to him, her voice not quite steady as she spoke his name. 'James, please!' Well aware of the kind of picture she made, she held out her arms briefly, then let them fall back against the slither of her nightdress. 'Please help me with this, the catch is so difficult.' A hand went up again, this time to lift her hair away from the nape of her neck, looking through her lashes in a way he would find deliberately provocative, 'James...' She turned her back so he was presented with a shoulder that was smooth and still retained some of the peachy bloom from their honeymoon. The nightdress dipped to the waist at the back and ...

'Tell me ...' When he reached her she could feel the warmth radiate from his body as he bent over, intent on the tiny silver clip. 'Tell me, Jane ...'

'Yes, darling?' She made a move, was halted by his sudden instruction but allowed her hand to drift against his arm.

'Keep still, darn you.' But it was a lazy, half-amused tone. 'There you are.' At last he disengaged the catch, cradling the bauble for a second in his palm before holding it out to her. 'Do you always keep your necklace on when you have a bath?'

Hardly aware of what he said, Jane stared up at him, her heart hammering so wildly against her ribs that almost everything else was blotted out, and with that dark face hovering above hers, lips slightly parted to show the white even teeth . . .

'No.' The whisper was automatic. She touched his chest, spreading out the fingers, rubbing so each nerve was picking up the forceful pulse below the surface and . . . 'No, not always.'

'Strange.' His voice was low like hers, and with a note that sent a tremor the length of her spine. 'Strange that the chain should be so bone dry.'

'Very.' The eyes looking up at him were dark, limpid with appeal, halfway between languorous invitation and . . . innocence, perhaps.

'Strange too,' his mouth was close to her cheek, she could feel his breath stir her hair, 'that you weren't wearing it at dinner.'

Her hands moved to his shoulders, linking behind his neck, pulling his face against hers. 'James,' it was a half-smothered supplication.

'Jane,' his mouth brushed against hers in the tantalising way she loved, his fingers moved aside the slender straps, his lips moved lower, lingering over the column of her throat. 'My darling. My devious little Jane,' his voice was rough, breathy, 'it's been so long.'

'Two whole days,' she whispered. 'Endless, endless days.' She stood on tiptoe, her lips barely in contact with his but aware of the length of that powerful body.

'And I promise you, I have no intention of waiting a moment longer. No matter what differences there are between us.' He swung her up in his arms, crossed the room and deposited her gently on the bed, where he stood looking at her for a minute, then sank on to the floor beside her. 'Feel this.' He reached out for her hand and placed it on his chest. 'You know what you're doing to me.'

'And this,' she held his hand against her breast, gave a tiny plaintive moan when his fingers moved aside the thin silk which was all that separated them. And then the lights were extinguished, leaving them in the soft darkness where their only experience was heady delight.

'Jane! Jane, my darling,' it was much later before he spoke, 'say you'll come with me. Say you'll come to Brazil. We'll have the most wonderful time there together.'

'Mmm.' Jane nuzzled against his shoulder, stretched out her hand and touched his chest, sighed deeply and curled up contentedly after another incoherent murmur.

James lay on his side and stared into the darkness. It was a long time before he fell asleep.

CHAPTER SIX

THANK heavens! The train was damp and steamy, smelling unpleasant after a day of coping with rain-soaked clothes. Jane sat in a corner, anxious to be home in time to have a quick bath. Thank heaven, she thought again, for Arthur and his invitation for this evening. Another night alone in the flat would be... She sighed deeply, and as no one noticed it was easy for her to slip into her familiar daydream. Nostalgia, it seemed, was all that kept her going these days.

In the two months since James had left, life had been mere existence, and although she loved her job and found it as stimulating as she had ever imagined, it wasn't enough. Something basic and essential was missing. It was such a loss that last Sunday she had spent the entire day wandering about the flat, going from room to room searching for... well, she didn't know quite what she was looking for.

Except... blindly she stared ahead of her, hardly prepared to admit it... it was all tied up with James and missing him so desperately. Nothing had prepared her for the pain of their separation. She had no resources, no experience to help her cope with it. Anyway—she drew in a shuddering breath—she had to make the best of it, get on with her life and try to accept the fact that up till now James had showed no sign of forgiving her.

'I'm asking you, Jane, to come with me to Brazil.' On his last night in London he had faced her across the table. His face was stern and strained, there was no relaxation about him, he wasn't influenced by the rather special bottle of wine, the meal over which she had slaved in a determination to make it so memorable, and he had certainly not even noticed the pink linen, the pale green candles with their romantic flicker. It would have been the same if she had pushed some frozen dinners into the microwave. 'If you stick to this ridiculous decision, what else can I think but,' here he shrugged as if already he had given up all hope, 'that your job is more important to you than our marriage?'

'Darling!' Throughout a frantic day, her brain had been spinning trying to find a way out, and it had been Lottie, still silently disapproving, who had made a tentative suggestion and who had then spent the afternoon on the telephone making enquiries on her behalf. 'I've been thinking—I got on to all kinds of travel firms today, and there's a possibility... Let's say I take a short leave in about six weeks? I could fly out to be with you.' She tried not to be discouraged by the impassive expression on his face. 'I could possibly tack on a weekend to make it more worthwhile. And then maybe in another three months I could take a long weekend and we could meet halfway. Think, James, we could book in at the Ocean Bay, it would be such fun going back there, and...' She faltered in the face of his lack of response. 'I know it would be expensive, but—well, what do you think?'

'You know exactly what I think. I'm not in the market for a part-time wife. I want you with me all the time. Not just popping across to spend an hour or two in bed, then back to London and Beaumont's feeling self-righteous that you've done your duty and now can get on with your real life for a bit.'

Now her face was every bit as white and strained as his. She had to struggle against the tears threatening to spill down her cheeks. It was hard to understand why he was being so unfair. 'That's your picture, but I see it rather differently. And at least I'm trying to do something about...'

'If you'd like to do something you can come to Brazil with me—it's quite simple.'

'Why are you being so pigheaded?' Her voice rose, anguished. 'We've been through it a hundred times. I've explained that I can't—I just can't leave Beaumont's at this moment, I——'

'Then when?' James interrupted cruelly and instantly. 'Give me a date, Jane, then maybe we can work something out.' The mouth which could be so tender, so deliriously gentle, was a taut gash. 'Tell me when you'll be ready to throw in your hand at Beaumont's.'

'I can't—you must see that. Oh, it would be easy, wouldn't it, just to invent a date and then I could find out later it wasn't suitable? But I'm trying to be honest with you.' Her voice was shaking with passion, her green eyes translucent with unshed tears. 'If we can't be honest with each other there isn't much hope for us.'

'No.' The word was spoken in a contemplative way, almost detached. 'No, maybe you're right. In any event,' he was looking at her as if he hardly knew her, 'I don't think there's a great deal more we can say to each other, do you?'

'James!' Jane felt as if her heart was being wrenched from her body. It was difficult for her to believe this was happening—to them, to her and James.

'Anyway,' a little impersonal smile, 'I have quite a bit of paperwork to sort out before my flight, and you must be tired, so I suggest you go and get some sleep. I might be some time.'

She stared at him, afraid to speak, afraid of bursting into tears if she opened her mouth, afraid of and for everything that was happening in her life right then. So without a word she turned away and began to clear the things from the table, scraping the amalgam of pheasant, chestnuts and cream from plates into the waste disposal, then stacking them in the dishwasher. Methodically she brushed up crumbs, pushing napkins and tablecloth into the laundry basket, carefully washing their best glasses and replacing them in the cupboard.

Then she did as James had suggested and went to bed, lying sleepless and staring in the dark as she waited for him to join her. Only when he did she found she couldn't do what she longed to do; she couldn't reach out and touch him in a gesture that might have been taken for apology. Not when he was so very much in the wrong. So she lay stiff and unyielding, waiting for him to make the first move, for him to circle her with his arms as he always did, so that even if they didn't make love they would be reminded that each was part of the other. But he simply switched off the light and, as far as she could judge, fell instantly asleep.

And in the morning he said he would prefer it if she didn't come to the airport to say goodbye, and she was too proud to tell him she had arranged to have the morning off specially for that purpose. He had kissed her on the mouth as if she were some kind of favourite cousin, mentioned in a matter-of-fact way the various financial arrangements he had made. She had interrupted then, meaning to be helpful and trying to stop the hurt that was inside her.

'James, please don't worry about that. I earn quite enough money to——'

'Ah, yes,' he swung round in the act of picking up his briefcase, bending his head as he began to undo the strap, 'that's what this is all about, isn't it?'

'Wh-what do you mean?' Even as she spoke the doorbell rang persistently.

'My transport, I think.' He put up a hand and rubbed her cheek with the back of his hand, his expression one of wry affection mingled with sadness. 'I mean,' he reverted to her query, 'young women of your generation, Jane, independent, successful, don't take kindly to being supported by a man. Take care of yourself, won't you? You're very special, always will...' Again the jarring ringing interrupted, the dark head turned impatiently in the direction of the door, and he sighed. 'This is it, then. Goodbye.' And he was gone.

Sitting in the train, Jane could quite easily remember the stab of quite incredible pain, the wave of total disbelief that very nearly submerged her. Until then, until that very instant, she hadn't really believed James would go. Something would happen, the plans for Brazil would in some miraculous way drift away, becoming one of those nightmarish things that nearly happened. But all at once she was alone, more lonely than she had ever been in her life before, and alone she had been ever since.

Which was why she was so grateful for some relief tonight. The train slowed. She rose, swung on the strap, looking back at her seat to check that she had everything. It was good of Arthur to have gone to such trouble to find tickets. The show had been billed as a sell-out for months, so heaven knew what they had cost him. And it wasn't as if light musicals were his kind of thing, but he seemed to sense that just now a night of grand opera was not likely to do much for her. And soon, in just about two weeks, she would be going down to spend Christmas with her parents, three whole days when she could rest and relax—except, she reminded herself, that she would have to invent a whole scenario of James's doings in Brazil.

He had, of course, written once or twice, airmail sheets packed with details of local conditions, much about a little cat which had adopted him as a surrogate parent and which had suddenly produced a litter of tiny kittens, all equally showing signs of intense cupboard love. Interesting letters if they had come from an elderly uncle, but coming from the man she loved... Jane had replied much in the same vein, telling him how busy she was at Beaumont's, describing in detail plans for going to Paris in the early part of the year to see the latest collections. All the minutiae of her life, which she supposed he would find deadly boring. It wasn't as if he had ever shown the least sign of interest in her career. A shaft of self-pity stabbed at her.

But one day, in a kind of desperate longing, one she felt could be stilled no other way, she had actually picked up the receiver and dialled the number of his bungalow. At the offices of Atlantic Oil they had been very sympathetic when she told them how she had accidentally mislaid it. Listening to it ringing, she put a hand over the palpitating beating of her heart and only then wondered what she was going to say when he answered, but then a woman's voice, low and sultry, came on the other end. Jane stammered out her request.

'James, honey,' the voice surely belonged to someone not much over twenty; she could just imagine her, dark and exotic, devastatingly attractive and...used to pleasing men. 'For you, James.' Then heels tapping on a tiled floor as she came back towards the telephone. 'Just a moment, please, he's in the bath just now, but he's coming.' But when James reached the telephone, the caller had gone, and it was assumed the call he had been expecting from his London office had been disconnected. Whereas Jane, tortured now with jealousy, made up her mind she would never ring him again. She ought to have noticed...he knew where she was, and all he had to do was lift the telephone and dial the number. That he had not troubled to do that said quite a lot...

She rushed into Tenterden House, through the hall and into the lift. Time was slipping away and she must be ready for Arthur. She caught sight of the porter emerging from his room and waved, but she had pressed the button by the time he called her name, indicating that he had some kind of message for her which would have to wait till she came down again.

She sighed as she opened the front door, threw her coat and handbag towards a chair in her bedroom, cast a glance at the clothes she had had the foresight to lay out on the bed this morning, then she reached for the tab of the zip at the back of her neck. By the time she reached the door of the shower-room she had already stepped out of her dress when she stopped dead, her attention caught by a slight noise. The hairs at her nape rose as she came to the conclusion that she wasn't alone; someone was in the flat with her.

A heavy hand mirror lay on the dressing-table, and she grabbed it, hesitated, before advancing to stand in the centre of the hall, turning till she identified the source of the sound as being her old bedroom, the one she had shared with James until she made up her mind the smaller one, the one with no memories attached, would suit her better for the time being. As she looked, she noticed the slip of light under the door. Her heart was bounding feverishly now and a flick in the direction of the wall mirror did little to reassure her. Such a display of bare flesh was at the least foolish, at the worst she might be inviting... She had almost made up her mind to make a dash for the door, throw it open and start yelling, when the one facing swung suddenly open and... a male figure dressed only in a scanty blue towel confronted her. His head was totally concealed by another towel being vigorously applied to wet hair, but it was a body of which she knew every inch and with an intimacy that brought a prickle of heat to her skin. At once her heart went into overdrive and in a completely different direction, joy and pleasure seared for a split second. It almost seemed as if her prayers had been answered.

It was a moment before he sensed he was no longer alone. He dropped the towel so it draped about his shoulders like a scarf and was looking at her, his dark eyes intent on her face, skimming over her bare shoulders and arms, then returning, more guardedly now, to her face, especially perhaps to her mouth, and she felt her lips part as her breathing grew more hurried. But there was something about his eyes now, a reserve which concealed those glinting amber lights, none of the encouragement she sought and which would have had her run forward, throw her arms about him.

'James!' Her legs all at once were weak. She subsided on to a chair and dropped her weapon on to the table close by. 'What on earth...?' Anger flooded her then, driving out the surge of joy and pleasure. 'You frightened me to death. You might have let me know.'

'I'm sorry.' His tone, she thought, discounted that. 'I thought Ted would have told you. Anyway, I didn't expect you so early. These aren't Beaumont's hours, as I remember.' He picked up the mirror, weighed and tested it thoughtfully. 'What did you mean to do with this?'

'What do you think I was going to do with it?' Surely it hardly needed explaining. 'I heard a noise, thought it had to be an intruder and decided I'd do my best to defend your possessions.'

'In that gear?' He raised a sceptical eyebrow. 'More like an invitation.'

'I *am* in my own home.' Realising that was a debatable point, Jane felt the colour rise in her cheeks. 'I can dress exactly how I like.' Disappointed, bitter, she got up and moved across to her room, walked inside trying not to notice that he had followed and was watching her cross to the bathroom door.

'I said,' he reminded her, and she knew he had noticed the gauzy chiffon dress, the filmy under-things spread out on the bed, 'these are not Beaumont's hours—at least, not as I remember them.' The implications of what he was saying caught her at once on the defensive.

'I . . .' She slipped her arms into her dressing-gown. Her mind was in a whirl. In less than half an hour Arthur would be arriving; he would be already on his way. 'I *was* going out this evening.'

'Well, I'm glad of that. Glad you haven't been sitting at home moping.' James turned and strode across the hall, and Jane followed, standing at the door of what was now his room while he disappeared into the bathroom, emerging almost at once belting his navy towelling robe about his waist. 'So long as you haven't been lonely.'

Lonely? What did he know about being lonely? Him and his...his woman! It would have been easy to scream out at him, to let him know in no uncertain tone that tonight was to have been her first outing in two months, since he had left, in fact, but instead she managed to speak calmly. This wasn't the time, not with Arthur due to arrive at any moment.

'I didn't expect you back, James. If I'd known do you really think . . . ?' Her mind was whirling with the problem—what could she tell Arthur when he came? There was no way she was going out with him now James was back, even if it was now almost a tradition that he took her somewhere special for Christmas.

'No.' His tone was flat, unapologetic, maybe even a little resentful. 'Well, I didn't know myself till a few days ago. It all came out of the blue. I did try to call you last night, but I couldn't get through.'

'Oh.' Still busy with the problem of Arthur, she took a second to remember that she had taken the phone off the hook and gone to bed early, but her mind moved on to something else. 'Is there a special reason for you coming back, James? It's a long way, unless . . .'

'You're right, it is a long way.' His dry tone was a comment on her not very original remark, but she was too intent on him to notice. She watched as he bent to accommodate his height at the dressing-table, raking the hair back from his face with a few sweeping moves of a comb. 'And you're right, there is a special reason.' He was watching her reflection carefully, seeing the colour come and go as her mind toyed with an idea. He undoubtedly knew exactly what she was thinking, how she was feeling, and his next words were brutally to the point. 'The company is being reorganised from the bottom up, and of course,' he swung round from the mirror and faced her, leaning back half supported by the corner of a chest of drawers, bare feet casually crossed at the ankles, 'certain people have been made redundant.'

Redundant? The word pierced her brain like an arrow. Again she had to suppress this almost over-whelming urge to rush forward, to wrap her arms about him, to comfort him in any way a wife might be expected to... but the longing was stifled by the expression on his face. Comfort from her was the last thing he wanted just now. 'Not you?' She shook her head. What kind of company would want to get rid of a man like James Barnard? 'They wouldn't make you redundant, James. They wouldn't.'

'Why not?' Bitterness was all around them as he lashed out, and she had the idea he had guided and planned their conversation till they reached that point where he could exact a revenge. 'After all, you did.'

She would rather, she assured herself when, shaking and shivering, she reached her own room, hurrying to fix necklace and earrings with in-capable fingers, she would much rather he had struck her.

Make-up applied automatically, a little heavy-handed by her normal standard but none the less... Jane stood back to check, thinking she looked passable. The sea-greens and blues of the dress suited her and if only, if only James had wanted her to be with him, to talk, nothing else, to listen, but he had thrown even that back at her when, reeling from the bitterness of the accusation, she had tried to remain cool, had managed after a long agonising minute to find a calm even voice to speak to him. 'I don't really want to go out tonight. You'll want something to eat and...'

'Please, don't think of changing your plans for me. Besides...' he paused.

'I told you I would prefer to cancel.'

'I'd much rather you didn't. In any case, I have someone coming round this evening. There are plans to be made for the future, and...'

'If that's how you feel.' It was difficult to believe this was happening. They were talking to each other like strangers.

'That is how I want it.' And he had turned and walked away from her.

When she emerged from her own room he was dressed in well washed, comfortable old jeans, navy shirt under a cotton knit pullover. He cast a mockingly approving glance in her direction. 'Must be something pretty special.'

'The new American musical.' What was the use of telling him that she had bought the dress with him in mind, knowing that he liked the colours and... 'James, I would still much prefer it if...' The house telephone interrupted just then, and James who was closest lifted the receiver. 'Hi, Ted.' The dark eyes were on his wife as he listened, did not move from her face, though he nodded once or twice. 'Right, I'll pass on the message. Goodbye.'

Jane hated the smile on his face, hated the bitterness of what wasn't truly a smile. There was neither light nor warmth in it. 'So it's Arthur, is it?' Again he took a leisurely inventory of every-

4 Free! Temptation romances

Plus a Free Teddy & Mystery Gift!

In heartbreak and in ecstasy Temptations capture all the bittersweet joys of contemporary romance.

And to introduce to you this powerful and fulfilling series, we'll send you *4 Temptation romances* absolutely **FREE** when you complete and return this card.

We're so confident that you'll enjoy Temptations that we'll also reserve a subscription for you, to our Reader Service, which means that you could enjoy...

- **4 BRAND NEW TEMPTATIONS -** sent direct to you each month (before they're available in the shops).

- **FREE POSTAGE AND PACKING -** we pay all the extras.

- **FREE MONTHLY NEWSLETTER -** packed with special offers, competitions, author news and much more...

Free Books and Gifts claim

Yes Please send me my 4 FREE Temptation romances together with my FREE gifts. Please also reserve a special Reader Service subscription for me. If I decide to subscribe, I will receive 4 superb new Temptations for just £7.00 every month, post and packing FREE. If I decide not to subscribe I shall write to you within 10 days. The FREE books and gifts will be mine to keep. I understand that I am under no obligation whatsoever. I may cancel or suspend my subscription at any time simply by writing to you. I am over 18 years of age.

1A3T

Name —————————————

Address —————————————

————————— Postcode —————————

Signature —————————————

MAILING PREFERENCE SERVICE

Mills & Boon Reader Service

FREEPOST

P.O. Box 236

Croydon

CR9 9EL

NO STAMP NEEDED

Send NO money now

thing about her, from the top of her glossy head
to the sea-green pumps with the gold buckles. And
there was no use pretending to herself that he hadn't
been aware of the scald of colour in her cheeks when
he had mentioned the name of her escort. He had
always had this suspicion of her relationship with
Arthur, reading more into it than had ever existed.
'The message is will you hurry. The traffic's thick
and you're already later than he'd planned.' He
turned away and picked up the pile of papers he
had been studying when she came in.

'James, I . . .' She had to make one last effort to
repair some of the misunderstandings.

'You'd best be off.' Absently he looked up at her.
'Oh, and please thank Arthur on my behalf. Tell
him it's a great relief to know that he's been prepared to keep you company while I've been away.'

CHAPTER SEVEN

IN SPITE of the sumptuous production, Jane's reactions were automatic. When the audience roared with delight she smiled, joined in the applause not noticeably late, exchanged an amused glance with Arthur when once or twice she emerged from her own private turmoil to find his eyes on her. Sherlock Holmes himself, she was convinced, would hardly have been aware of her abstraction.

'It's been a lovely evening, Arthur.' Driving back to the flat, she injected the right degree of enthusiasm into her voice, then, solely because it was what good manners demanded, she heard herself inviting him up for coffee as they drove past the park on the last corner.

'Oh, I don't think I ought to—it's quite late enough already, and Mother tends to worry. You're quite a bit further out here, aren't you?'

'I'm sorry, Arthur,' now that attention had been drawn to it she was very aware of her thoughtlessness and overcome with guilt, 'I should have arranged for a taxi—dragging you all this way. You're sure I can't persuade you?' Certain now of his refusal, she felt it safe to press a little. 'James would be so pleased . . .'

'I'm sure James will be only too anxious to have you to himself. I know...' the lightness in his tone couldn't entirely conceal his wistfulness, 'I know I should be.'

'Thank you, Arthur.' When he drew up outside Tenterden House Jane leaned over and dropped a kiss on his cheek. 'It's been a wonderful evening. I always know Christmas is near when we've had our outing to the theatre.' She reached for the door-handle. 'I still don't know how you came by those tickets—bribery, I suspect!'

His laugh was coy, her vague accusation of raffishness pleasing to a man who throughout his life had never deviated from the conventional and proper. 'Not quite that—there are ways and means, you know. Now off you go. I don't want James to appear demanding to know why I've kept you out so late.'

'He won't do that,' she assured him. 'I think I told you he was expecting a colleague, so they'd be locked in weighty business discussions. Since he was busy himself he was grateful I was being looked after. Goodnight, Arthur, thank you.'

At first, in spite of glowing lamps in the hall, she thought she had the flat to herself, but then she heard a faint laugh and the soft murmur of voices, maybe even a backdrop of music emanating from the sitting-room. Or was the show's hit song still echoing in the back of her mind?

Quietly she went to her bedroom, disposing of her coat, checking her appearance, but in spite of her conclusion that she looked pale and colourless she took no steps to remedy matters. She was too tired, physically and emotionally, to make the effort. If James had one of his oil contacts she was in no mood to fill the role of perfect hostess. She was fit only to put her head round the door, make the right friendly sounds and disappear as soon as was convenient.

Pushing open the door, she took in the familiar scene, the dark head above the sofa positively inviting her to do what would have been entirely natural and instinctive a short time before—to go forward, lean her cheek against his, put her arms about his neck and . . . and ask him to forgive her.

The idea was so unexpected, such a shock, she was momentarily stunned. Her eyes blurred with tears as she realised how desperately she loved him. The course open to her was so clear and obvious that she couldn't think why it hadn't come to her before. She would ask him to forgive her. He must be feeling so bruised, wounded. She knew how she would feel in the same situation, if Beaumont's should ever find out they could do without her . . . But now she had him back, it was what she had been praying for all along, and she asked for nothing more from life than that he should be with her in their lovely flat.

And oh—for the first time she realised, and it brought a stab of positive relief—as things had turned out it was as well she hadn't given up her job in Beaumont's. Now she was in a position to support both of them should it be necessary. Not that she would breathe a word on the subject; she knew how touchy James could be. She *was* learning.

The ideas comforted her. She gave a tiny shuddering sigh, smiling as she caught sight of her reflection, her sea-green dress light and floaty, a romantic dress, the kind he had always loved seeing her wear. A step closer and then a second shock, as searing as the first and certainly more unwelcome, for now she could see what she had allowed to slip her mind. The colleague James had mentioned was entirely at home, curled up beside him on the sofa. In her *own* preferred position. And very female.

A step backwards, fingers on the door-handle as she closed it with a very decided click which brought James's head up so that this time their eyes met in the glass, clashed, his smile automatic, very fixed and artificial. And her response was hostile. She was remembering the accusation he had thrown at her before she left earlier in the evening, the torment it had caused her, how foolish she had been to let her tender feelings, her desire for reconciliation to allow her to weaken.

'Jane!' He stood and faced her then, voice and manner mild in a way she had almost forgotten and doubtless, she reminded herself, assumed purely to impress his...his 'colleague'.

'I didn't hear you come in.'

'No,' her eyes flashed, as she determined next time he must be the one to... 'I realise that. I'm sorry if I'm interrupting.' She turned as the female uncurled herself from the settee. Her face felt frozen, but she was able to produce a semblance of interest as he introduced them.

'My wife Jane. Darling, you haven't met Miranda de Mowbray—she's been my right hand all the time I've been with Atlantic. But I've spoken about her, so you know how important she is.'

And the moment she spoke, mouthing all the platitudes in that liquid exotic accent, Jane placed her exactly, and simmered with rage that James had brought her here to his—no, to *their* home. She had been right to suspect the worst. A wave of sick jealousy overtook her. She had been wrong to talk herself out of her suspicions after that impulsive telephone call to Brazil. In her determination to be fair to James, she hadn't wanted, for heaven's sake, to believe he was having an affair, and just because a woman had a sultry sexy voice it didn't necessarily mean . . .

In one respect at least—— She forced herself to calm down, to subdue the inner turmoil. In one respect she had been wrong. The tall voluptuous creature of her imagination with flashing eyes and a tempestuous manner turned out to be small and slight, although, given cause, the black eyes could doubtless flash extravagantly. And now that she was closer, the observation caused a stab of quite unworthy satisfaction. Miranda de Mowbray was older than she had first thought; the network of tiny lines about the eyes spoke more of forty than thirty.

But she was attractive and elegant in a casual sort of way. The leisure suit she was wearing was plain, but there was no deceiving an expert like Jane. Tucked somewhere inside was a designer label, and velvet, the most luscious colour of crushed mulberry, a wonderful foil for her olive skin and black hair.

Still, now that some of her inner tensions were fading, she didn't think that James would find her... On the other hand, propinquity sometimes produced strange bedfellows. Jane couldn't think what had caused her to use such a word, it hadn't been in her mind. She swallowed the lump in her throat. But supposing...they had known each other a long time, suppose...long before she and James had met...

They looked right together, that small woman who came just to his shoulder and James. Jane persisted in turning the knife in her own heart. They were at ease with each other, good friends as well as... She coloured when she realised she was being studied with an interest equalling her own, then both women looked at James when he made the standard enquiries about her evening.

'A wonderful show!' The display of enthusiasm helped to ease her bitterness. 'Very colourful, and brilliant music, as you'd expect.'

'And how was Arthur? Arthur,' James turned to his colleague as if he were sharing a private joke with her, 'Arthur Davis is the financial whizz-kid of Beaumont's publishing house.'

Inwardly furious, Jane ignored him. How dared he? Arthur, when all was said and done, was exactly what he appeared to be, a colleague and friend. She smiled at Miranda—of all the pretentious names. 'Are you fond of music?' Then she looked from one to the other as both laughed.

'That,' James waved a hand in the direction of their stereo, drawing her attention to the subdued sound, 'is Miranda on tape.' He turned up the volume so the persuasive beat became discernible as a guitar and vocal combination, a throbbing sensuous rhythm with undertones of flamenco, just the kind of thing Jane might have imagined the other woman would produce. At the same time she determined not to notice that the voice, though almost harsh in some of the passages, could switch to hauntingly beautiful tones in the flick of an eye.

'What a pity,' she couldn't have said what possessed her, jealousy most likely, 'you didn't bring your guitar with you.' She flashed a brilliantly insincere smile. 'We might have had a party. Now, I'll make some coffee for us all, shall I?'

Waiting for the kettle to boil, she felt her heart beating in agitation, though it was hard to explain why. She was placing the cafetière on a thread of heat when she heard James follow her into the kitchen. From the corner of her eye she saw him lounge in the doorway and for the first time acknowledged that her agitation was a straight reflection of nervousness. She threw a glance over her shoulder. 'Does she take sugar, do you know?'

If her voice wasn't completely steady she didn't think he noticed.

'If you ever,' he took a step closer, making her hand shake as she spooned coffee into the jug, 'speak to a guest like that again——'

'A guest?' Skirts flared out about her legs as she whirled round accusingly. 'And I thought you were expecting a colleague!' Her green eyes were brilliant with emotion. Remembering that wash of sentimentality when she first arrived back, she felt humiliated by her own weakness. To think she had been about to...

'Anyone who comes into this house is a guest, no matter what the purpose of their visit, but it's a simple fact that we've been trying to get to grips with some radical problems since eight o'clock. Miranda has given up her own time to help me with it.'

With a sudden qualm Jane remembered what she had barely noticed earlier—the long low coffee table in front of the sofa *had* been scattered with computer print-outs, on the floor to one side she imagined there had been a lap-top processor, and...

'And if you're ever rude to a guest again...'

'I don't agree that I was rude.' Maybe flippant, she told herself defensively, but...

'As close to being rude as makes little difference.' James turned away, looking back at her for a second. 'And yes, she does take sugar. Cream too, if it isn't too much trouble.'

Now who's rude? Jane asked herself as she strode back and forth across the kitchen, banging cups on to saucers, rather resenting having to open the pack of specially delicious biscuits she had bought with Arthur in mind. But by the time she returned to the sitting-room she had got her thoughts under control again, determined to be as charming as she knew how, asking all kinds of pertinent questions concerning music and how it fitted in with Miranda's work at Atlantic.

'If you want to go to bed, darling——' James looked up from the piles of papers which had regained most of his attention while the women chatted, and his tone caused Jane's head to jerk towards him. She felt her face grow hot, something she knew the other woman was bound to notice even though her husband was oblivious. And she did take a second to consider if the endearment, so casually, tenderly uttered, had been chosen specially to conceal the real state of their marriage. 'Miranda and I,' he went on, 'still have some ends to tie up.' Maybe the silence attracted his attention, for he shot a sudden dark glance upwards and smiled at her, that lazy appreciative smile that would always have the power to make her feel she was dropping twenty storeys down a lift shaft. 'I know you have to be up at the crack of dawn. Jane,' he explained to his colleague, 'has a very demanding job.'

'All right,' instead of throwing her cup at him as her see-saw, unpredictable emotions now seemed to be suggesting, Jane began to collect the things together on to the tray, 'if you're sure you don't mind.' She smiled at Miranda as if she meant it and got to her feet. 'It's been so nice—maybe we'll meet again some time.' Pretty unlikely, in present circumstances.

'Sure to.' The woman spoke in total confidence—surprising, Jane thought in the circumstances, but then James had implied that until his contract ended on the last day of the month no one at Atlantic had any idea… As she reached the door she found Miranda there opening it for her, looking at her with a very knowing lift of the eyebrows, an expression of conjecture in her dark eyes.

Well, who could blame her? As she stacked the cups into the dishwasher Jane couldn't subdue the bitterness that rose again, an implacable tide inside her. Who wouldn't be surprised at such behaviour from a young healthy male just that day returned from Brazil? So immersed in his pages of figures that he could quite blandly send his new—comparatively new; Jane allowed herself one tiny sob before catching her lips between her teeth—send his wife to bed while he dallied for hours with his secretary or whatever she pretended to be.

Hours later she heard carefully lowered voices before the front door closed with a subdued click, hall lights were extinguished and the flat was dark, silent, lonely as it had ever been over the last two months.

For the next two days she barely saw James— partly her own fault, as she did make an effort to be up and away from the flat especially early, and the imminence of Christmas made a convenient excuse should he enquire. Which he didn't. Most likely he was as pleased as she to avoid unnecessary confrontation. Besides, he was so involved himself.

By chance they met for a cup of tea on the second afternoon when Jane came home early and found James still there, sitting at the kitchen table and absorbed by the usual sheaf of papers.

'Hi,' as she spoke he looked up, seemed to recognise her and went to fetch another mug, 'I've just made some tea—sit down and have a cup.' He pushed aside a chair for her with the toe of a polished shoe.

'Thanks,' she sighed, threw off her jacket and took his advice, suppressing a groan of weariness. She had been on her feet all day, strap-hanging on the crowded train home, and was just about all in. Under cover of the table she eased her aching feet from her shoes and sipped gratefully at the scalding brew. 'I thought——' She tried to keep the edge of resentment from her voice, but he looked so very freshly showered, so immaculate in a dark grey suit she hadn't seen before, pale shirt, silk tie in shades of maroon and grey, so entirely wholesome as if in contrast to her dreary black and white, stale and in need of a long soak. She had trapped her fingers in a metal drawer just as she was leaving and her nail varnish was chipped and tacky. As fresh as last week's news, in fact. 'I thought as you've been made redundant you wouldn't have such a work-load.'

'Mmm.' The glance in her direction was ab-stracted, then, clearly reaching a decision, he bundled the papers together and began to push them into his briefcase. 'Mmm, yes, I suppose it does seem odd, but there are always ends to be tied up. I want to leave my desk clear before I finish with my present job, and naturally...' he paused, looking at her thoughtfully for a moment '...contacts to be made for...whatever lies ahead.' He got to his feet, adjusted his tie a little and turned away. 'Oh, by the way...'

'Yes?' She was still resentful and disinclined to disguise the fact.

'Your mother rang just before you arrived home.'

'Oh?' In the act of rising to take her mug to the sink, Jane sat down again with a bump. That was something she had been postponing since his return, something that had been causing her sleepless nights. Exactly how was she going to put her parents in the picture? Would it be possible over Christmas to hide the fact that James was back in London, or should she prepare them...?

'She didn't seem to realise I was back,' he added. 'She sounded rather surprised.'

'Of course she'd be surprised. I haven't had time to contact her.'

'And delighted. And naturally she and your father are expecting me to join the family party for Christmas.'

'So...' Stunned by the turn of events, Jane looked at him. 'So,' she repeated more forcefully, 'what did you say? What excuse did you make?'

'Excuse?' His voice and eyes were cool, challenging as he stood looking at her. 'It didn't occur to me that there was any need to make an excuse. I thanked her and said I was looking forward to it.' A glance at his watch and he picked up his briefcase. 'I must go, or I'll be late.'

'James, you can't go like that!' she protested. 'It's going to be an impossible situation. I don't want them to be upset, and...'

'Leave it for now, will you, Jane?' There was a sudden weariness about him that pulled at her, even found an echo in her own feelings. For the first time she was conscious that beneath the tanned exterior was a man who must be edgy and tired—but did men like James Barnard ever feel tired? 'The last thing I want is to worry your parents, and we must talk, I agree, but not now. Let's leave it till after Christmas, that shouldn't be too difficult for either of us, and after that we'll make time. We can keep up a pretence for their sakes. I feel I owe them that even more than you do.' He paused, she felt her eyes fill with unexpected tears and jumped up, busying herself at the sink in an effort to hide them. 'What do you say?' He had come up and was standing close.

'All right.' In control again, she turned, a teacloth in her hand as she rubbed industriously at the mug.

'Good girl.' The hint of approval, even of gentleness, took her by surprise, and she turned again, biting feverishly at her lip. 'Then after Christmas, as soon as we have time to draw breath,' she felt the touch of his hand against the back of her neck, in other times it might have been a caress; there was a smile in his voice as he went on, 'I'll let you get over the trauma of Paris first and then, I promise, we'll work something out. It will be perfectly amicable, you have my word.' Again a finger stirred against the soft downy texture of her skin, and it was hard not to call out. 'All right?' And she nodded, unable to risk opening her mouth in case she made a complete fool of herself. 'Perfectly amicable'—the words echoed inside her head long after he had gone. There was a menacing ring to them; hard to say why, till she remembered how often they were used to describe a friendly divorce...not that she could believe there was such a thing.

On the Saturday evening before Christmas she came back late to find the flat empty, and it seemed to make her gesture of buying some boxes of glittery decorations particularly pointless. Already James had been away for two nights, and she had been hoping that tonight... But there, she imagined he was trying to establish as many contacts as he could so that when his redundancy actually took effect he would be as well placed as possible. It was still hard to understand what Atlantic Oil was thinking about—but it was happening all around these days.

For a few minutes Jane sat glancing at the paper, dithering about making a proper meal, but she had eaten at lunchtime and it would be easier to make do with coffee and sandwiches. Besides, she didn't think she could face another supper on her own. She was reaching into the fridge for a pack of smoked salmon when quite unexpectedly the doorbell rang. She found herself running through the hall, her heart going wild in anticipation before she had time to tell herself that of course it would not be James. He always had his own door-key, coming and going at all hours made him more insistent that he didn't want to disturb her, but still...

At least she was able to hide the worst of her disappointment when she found Miranda de Mowbray on the doorstep. She was wearing figure-hugging leopard-patterned pants and clutching a short velvet jacket about her, and she smiled, the usual dazzle of teeth against dark skin. 'Thank goodness!' Following Jane's gesture, she stepped inside. 'James was by no means sure you'd be at home, he didn't know if you had anything planned, so it's nice to find you in.' Since she never went anywhere these days that remark was enough to rub one up the wrong way, Jane thought as she led the way into the sitting-room. And then, for no logical reason, she experienced a stab of anxiety.

'James is all right, isn't he?'

'James is fine.' If Miranda hadn't been rummaging in the large bag she had parked on the sofa beside her she might have noticed that such casual

enthusiasm didn't delight his wife. She produced a
notebook. 'Only there are some papers he must
have urgently, and he's sent me for them.'

'I see.' Humiliating having to admit so much to
this woman, but Jane felt entitled to know. 'Where
have you come from?'

'I've flown down from Aberdeen—company jet.
We'll be taking off again as soon as I pick up these
documents.'

'I see.' Jane hesitated. 'I don't suppose you've
time for a coffee? I've just made some.' Difficult
to understand her offer; she wasn't *that* lonely.

'Coffee would just about save my life, and there's
bound to be a delay while they refuel and so on.
James...' Miranda studied her notebook, rummaged inside her bag again and produced some
outsize spectacles. 'That's better—I can see now.
James says will you hand over a green file marked
25D, third drawer from top right in his desk in the
study? And in the meantime, please may I use your
loo?'

By the time she reappeared Jane had the coffee
things ready, the file on the table which Miranda
immediately stowed inside her bag. 'This is good!'
She drank thirstily, refused a biscuit and sat back
with a deeply-felt sigh of relief. 'I've been on the
go since I got up this morning—even on the plane
I was typing out analyses. There are times when I
feel quite homesick for Brazil. It seems a much more
relaxed way of life there.' A slight shrug and she
smiled. 'You wouldn't think I had a drop of Anglo-

Saxon blood, though my father's family come from Leicestershire.'

'So you consider Brazil your real home, do you?' In spite of herself Jane couldn't help being drawn to the woman. Now that they had met she no longer seemed such a threat, and there was something lively and attractive about her.

'Well, I was born in Mexico City, my mother's home, but as Dad was in oil we seemed always to be on the move—but certainly I think of myself as South American, even though the parents are settled in the States. Yes, please,' she held out her cup when Jane offered a refill. 'Mmm, when I finish this I must run—no, there's something about Brazil, it just seems to suit me. Maybe it's the music.' Raising her hands in the air, she clicked imaginary castanets. 'I can't say, but I simply love the place. Especially Rio. It's a pity you couldn't make it, Jane, you would have had a wonderful time. Such a shame, when it was one of the few postings for a married man—they're by no means as common as you might think, even in a company as large as Atlantic. On the other hand, I do see it from your point of view. I'm keen enough on my own career. Now,' she looked at the clock on the mantelpiece, 'I must fly. Oh, and,' she paused with her hand on the doorknob, 'James said to give you his love.' She raised an eyebrow, shrugged in a very Latin way and was gone before Jane thought to ask when she might expect her husband back.

On her own, she was aware of an indefinable sense of uneasiness. It wasn't mere annoyance at discovering that James had obviously discussed their private business with Miranda—after all, he would have felt obliged to offer some explanation. She returned to the sitting-room, switched on the television out of habit rather than any interest she had in the programme, then was reaching out for the mute button.

Something about Miranda, something she had said—and yet the woman had been perfectly amiable, normal in her manner, unthreatening. Even the accent was less affected now that her ear had grown accustomed to it. 'Eet's a peety you couldn't make eet, Jane' and 'James said to geeve you hees love.' What was it she had said, for heaven's sake? There had been some implication that had wakened all kinds of uneasy feelings...

And then, abruptly, something in her mind switched on to the actual words which were causing such mental discomfort. 'You would have had a wonderful time...one of the few postings for a married man.' A married man, not a bachelor...

Yes, that was it. For a second or two she thought of them, unable to interpret the significance of the threat they seemed to be exerting, and then they hit her with lacerating effect as she faced up to the unpalatable truth. It was all too much of a coincidence—their hurried marriage, James's impatience, insistence that he wanted something more than a fleeting affair.

She gave a little mew of protest, took up one of the soft cushions and wrapped her arms about it, then her mind was racing away, back to that night in the Caribbean when he told her he was due to move on the next day. In their anguish they had kicked off their shoes and walked along the shore with the water lapping over their toes, arms about each other, stopping to kiss with a kind of frantic desperation and at last leaving the lights of the hotel far behind.

'There's only one solution to the problem, then, isn't there, my darling?' Light from the full moon had turned the planes of his face to silver, as he hovered above her, hawkish and dominating, more like pagan god than man at that moment. And at the same time his fingers had found the gap where her skirt had parted from her blouse and were moving sensuously over the skin.

'Wh-what do you mean?' Jane had shivered from the strength of her reactions, lifting her mouth to his, brushing, teasing.

'I mean we must get married—now. Or at least no later than tomorrow.'

'James!' Utter joy with just a sprinkling of fear had raced through her veins. 'Must we wait till tomorrow? Why not now?' His hands had moved to circle her waist and she thought she would faint from the sensation. 'Here, James. And now.'

'No,' he had whispered against her ear, his fingers stopping their delicious, provocative enticement, 'not here. When it happens between us for the first time it must be perfect, not,' his brief tense laugh had been calculated to restore them to some kind of sanity, 'not gritty and spiky, but if you promise to marry me in...let's say the next few days, I promise it will be as perfect as I can make it.'

As it had been. Jane gave a great sob now, looked down at the cushion she was holding and threw it from her. He had made it quite, quite perfect for her. For him too, she had thought. But now—a tiny thread of suspicion—had he made up his mind even before they met that he wanted that job in Brazil? The job that required a man to be married.

It was all too much for her. Impatiently she brushed away the tears from her cheeks. She refused to think about it any more. But even as she made up her mind on that, another idea slipped in to worry her. Had he lost his job because she had chosen to stay behind, because he had not been able to produce a wife as required? Was that what he had meant when he threw that accusation at her, when he said with so much bitterness that *she* had made him redundant? And if that was the case then was it likely that he could ever forgive her?

CHAPTER EIGHT

BY MORNING Jane's mind was completely clear. A sleepless night had given her time to work it out to her own conviction, and even if she hated the result it was best to face the truth. James had known of the Brazil job when they met, and as he was ambitious—all those disclaimers early on were probably just sops to his own conscience—there would have been an irresistible attraction for him. That was why he had continued to press and entice.

'My love,' it was easy to remember, so easy; Jane felt again the familiar shudder of her body's response to the drift of his fingers against her face, 'what I want for us is nothing as ephemeral as an affair. Hush!' As she went to speak his hand had sealed her lips, he was smiling down at her, soft tropical darkness was all about them and she was completely at the mercy of her feelings. 'Hush, my darling! I'm determined to give you no time to think of any objections—you see, what I've just suggested is so impetuous it would be crazy for anyone else, but for us, such special people, it's gloriously and dramatically right.'

As if she would have dreamed of putting up objections even if she had thought of any. When her whole being had been clamouring for him, ob-

118

jection was the last thing in her mind, and this wildly unconventional act would underline all that was so intense and arresting about their love. He was right, there *was* something special about them, and marrying this way was the only means of showing it.

He too, she had no doubts about it, had been swept along just as fiercely by emotional demands as she. Nothing would convince her that it was entirely an economic decision on his side, but from now on, always at the back of her mind would be that little doubt; if it hadn't been for the prospect of a senior appointment in Brazil, would he have been quite content with a holiday affair? After all, she had made it more than clear how willing she was... In any case, he ought to have talked it over with her, given her the chance to express her opinion. If he had she would have made it perfectly clear how important her own ambitions were—and they could have had an idyllic two weeks...

Tears, the tears she had thought were all spent in last night's paroxysms, threatened again, so she began with unusual energy to cope with her normal weekend jobs round the flat. She tidied the wardrobe and chest of drawers in her room, tasks outside the scope of the contract cleaners who came in every day. Coming upon the box of Christmas decorations she had carried home the previous day, she looked at it in dismay for a moment before thrusting it away behind some cases in the boxroom, then, because she could no longer avoid it, she set about wrapping the last of her Christmas gifts, those she would take with her when they went down to her parents on Christmas Eve—something she was dreading. And never, she assured herself with a return of self-pity, never in her entire life had she looked forward to the festive season with so little pleasure.

And that reflection might have affected her response when picking up the telephone she heard her husband's voice at the far end of a crackly line. 'Jane, it's James here.'

'Oh, yes?'

'I'm still in Aberdeen and look like being tied up for a day or two yet. Oh, and thanks for finding those papers for Miranda...'

'She got back safely, did she?' Her opinion of Miranda was still see-sawing madly, and right now she felt satisfyingly bitchy. 'So much executive travel must be so tiring.'

'Well, you'll know all about that.' The voice that had been fairly neutral when he first spoke now had an abrasive edge to it.

'Oh, I wouldn't call the Jubilee Line noticeably executive,' said Jane drily.

'No?' James paused so long she understood he was reminding her exactly whose choice tied her to the boredom of daily underground travel. 'Well, not to worry, soon you'll be off on your own particular flings, so you needn't envy Miranda. I'm sure Paris will be much more glamorous than anything she's likely to encounter. Anyway,' he went on so swiftly she had no time to throw back his charge of jealousy, 'the reason I rang is to let you know I'm uncertain if I'm going to be free till late on Christmas Eve, so as you finish at midday I suggest you go down to your parents by train and we'll meet there.' He paused, and when she didn't speak, 'Are you still here, Jane?'

'Yes, I got the message.' No point in explaining that a brief prayer of thankfulness had delayed her reply. The shorter the time they spent with her parents, the less the strain as far as she was concerned, and maybe, if she kept her fingers crossed... 'Late Christmas Eve, you say? Have you any idea exactly how late?'

'Might be near ten, but don't hold up anything for me. I'll most likely have eaten, and if there's any change of plan I'll ring you there direct.'

'Yes, that'll be fine.' Tears were close again, and she had to struggle with her voice. The last thing she wanted was for James to realise just how miserable she was, and if she were to blurt out something which would give him a clue...

'Everything all right at Beaumont's?' For a second she imagined a trace of wistfulness, homesickness even—well, it was that time of year. 'Christmas sales breaking all previous records?'

'About fifty per cent up on last year.' The news which ought to have been so satisfying seemed just then to have lost some of its importance.

'You must be pleased.'

'Well, of course some of it's down to Maggie Devere, but...'

'Yes, I suppose so. I'll have to go, Jane, someone's on the other line. See you in Sussex if not before. Goodbye.'

And, as she hauled out the ironing-board and began to get her clothes ready for the next day, Jane found it difficult to avoid the speculation—for a man who had been made redundant, James appeared to have remarkably little free time.

Christmas Eve, in contrast with the previous ten days of damp cold drizzle, was brisk and sunny, in spite of a cool little breeze coming in off the sea, and after her father had met Jane at the station, and they had had a sandwich and a cup of coffee, he suggested a short walk across the Downs. 'Look at that dog!' he persuaded her. 'We're stuck with him till Edgar and Mollie come back, and I want him to have a good time.' The golden retriever sat grinning in front of him, as full of anticipation as if they had rattled the lead in front of his eyes.

'Almost like old times.' Nancy leaned forward and ruffled his head. 'Remember how Bran used to be so crazy for walks? The moment you got up out of a chair his tail started thumping on the carpet.'

'Yes.' There was a lump in Jane's throat as she thought about the mongrel they had rescued from the dogs' home, nostalgia for a time when life had been simpler and less emotional, though it had broken her heart when Bran died of a heart attack, and was buried under an apple tree in the back garden.

'Have you and Mum ever thought of having another dog?' she asked as she and her father walked briskly up through the lightly wooded country she paused to throw a stick for Joss, who chased wildly after it and returned almost immediately, laying the stick encouragingly at Jane's feet, barking.

'No. Your mother isn't very keen, especially now I'm about to retire. I suppose it is silly tying ourselves down, especially if we decide to travel.' They turned along a minor trail which would lead them directly back home. 'It's more like something you and James will be thinking of soon.'

'Oh, no,' Jane answered almost too quickly, then put out a gloved hand to catch at some overhanging branches, slipping them through her fingers, enjoying the resinous scent. 'It would be impossible in the flat.'

'Well, you won't be living in the flat for ever, will you? At least, I have the impression that some time James would like to settle in the country, and now he's home from Brazil...'

'It's too early to be making plans. Brr!' With determination she changed the subject. 'Thank goodness we're almost home—surprising how chilly it is when the sun goes in. Now, this is the last time, Joss.' She bent to pick up the proffered stick.

'I'm just going to have a smoke before I go in. Your mother's trying to persuade me to cut down and if she doesn't see me...' Her father paused at the corner, putting his lighter to his pipe and puffing vigorously once or twice before moving on. 'Hello, looks as if we've got a visitor.' And Jane, diverted from throwing what she promised Joss was the very last stick, stood stock still as she looked at the long rakish lines of a car she knew very well indeed.

'A lovely surprise!' Her mother appeared in the doorway. Behind her the hall was softly lighted, expertly decorated with swags of greenery coming down the staircase, each few feet nipped in with a scarlet satin bow. 'James has managed to get away—he's just putting his case up in the bedroom.' Even as she spoke the tall figure began to descend, moving with the easy grace so much part of him and which, in spite of all the defences Jane assumed, still affected her. Dressed in casual wear, beige trousers, pale cream sweatshirt, he still exuded that air of power and confidence she had noted the very first day at the airport.

'Hello, darling.' As she stepped across the doorway, he put his hands on her shoulders and bent his head, touching her cheek with his. Not exactly a kiss, she noticed, but close enough to deceive any onlooker. 'You see, I did what you asked.' His act continued, he stood back smiling; it was all most convincing. 'I made a tremendous effort and got away early. My,' he tested her cheek with the back of his hand, 'you feel cold. Come on inside and warm up.'

'It's just my face.' Jane unwound the long wool scarf from her neck, unzipped her anorak and moved to the cloakroom to hang them away. Her cheeks were cold, and now she could see in the mirror she realised how the breeze had brought the colour... at least, maybe it was something to do with the shock of seeing James when she didn't expect him. More colour flared when behind her she saw him lounge in the doorway, but she refused to catch his eye.

'You suit that shade.' In spite of her determination she flicked a glance, brief but enough to be disturbing. A hand went up to the neckline of the butter-yellow jumper as she tried to shut out the tall powerful figure, but it wasn't easy.

It was true what he said, though, the colour was good for her, and it picked up the yellow overcheck in her navy tartan trousers and... She smiled in relief now as her mother emerged from the kitchen with a teatray. 'You want a hand with that, Mum?'

'I just thought we could all do with something to take us through till supper.'

'Let me, Nancy, you lead on.' James reached out for the tray, smiling at his mother-in-law who, Jane noticed with unaccustomed asperity, was looking back with the most besotted expression. It was too much for her.

'I'll go and call Dad,' she practically accused the other two, 'I'm sure he'll be as much in need of tea as anyone else.'

Supper turned out to be a reasonably pleasant meal, and if Jane was rather quiet at least her parents seemed not to notice. They were both too busy being delighted with the recent addition to their family. And sitting opposite him did have its bitter-sweetness, and she had to be firm over that. It would have been so easy to allow herself to be beguiled as she listened to the story of James's upbringing in India, where his parents were medical workers. He was, after all, a very persuasive and fiendishly attractive man.

'So sad for you, James,' her mother started to remove the soup plates, 'so sad when you were hoping they'd be back in England before long...'

'Yes,' he sighed, and sparing a surreptitious glance, Jane saw his eyes were lowered, the long lashes like tiny fringes of silk against his skin. She longed, with all her heart she longed to rise, to go round the table and pull his head against her breast in a gesture of long-delayed comfort. 'At the time...' He shrugged, raised his eyes, saw her watching, and she was struck by the coldness in his expression which seemed to be directed exclusively at her. Instinctively her hand went to her throat in a gesture of vulnerability, she blinked, and when he registered again his eyebrow was raised in an expression she saw as patronising, and for a time she was so involved in her own pain she heard next to nothing of the conversation.

'Lovely trout, Mum.' She made the remark in the hope that no one would notice that she had ac-

cepted the smallest quantity, that she had merely
toyed with one tiny potato.

'Yes, Nancy, delicious.' Of course James would
have to butt in. 'I particularly liked the lemon
butter; I don't think I've had that before.'

'I'm glad you enjoyed it. We always have something simple on Christmas Eve, and as the freezer's
full of fish since Alan had such a good season...'
Nancy got to her feet and began with Jane to clear
plates and serving dishes. 'Will you bring in the
pudding, dear? It's just,' she apologised to James,
'meringue or bread and butter pudding.'

'I have very fond memories of your bread and
butter pudding, Nancy, so I'll stake my claim right
now. I promise you,' as Jane reached the kitchen
she had to strain her ears to make it out, 'if I'd met
you before Jane I'd have earmarked her as my wife
on the strength of your bread and butter pudding
alone!' Moving away out of earshot, clattering
china as she rinsed plates under the tap, Jane made
no attempt to damp down the wave of bitterness
that swept through her. What next? First the
prospect of a job in Brazil, then a girl whose mother
could cook bread and butter pudding, for heaven's
sake—the sheer crassness of her thoughts didn't
strike her just then... But love, first and last el-
ement in *her* decision to marry, where did love come
in to James's equation? And she didn't know if she
wanted to hear the answer to that one or not.

'Bread and butter pudding.' Mindful of her role,
she had her smile so firmly fixed that her face ached

with the effort. She put the dishes down in front of her mother. 'Meringue and cream.' She sat without as much as a glance at the man opposite. 'Maybe it's time you gave me some lessons—I've never made a bread and butter pudding in my life.'

'Time enough for that, dear,' placidly her mother spooned the delicious mixture into plates, 'when you decide to give up work at Beaumont's.' And she didn't seem to notice the look of long-suffering on her daughter's face.

Later, the Scrabble board was produced. It was taken for granted that all would join in, and Jane had no satisfactory excuse ready, so once again she was sitting in a position where it was difficult to avoid looking at her husband. She twisted round in her chair, yawned once or twice, forgot when it was her turn to play, patted the dog's head, then had to be nudged.

'I thought it was your turn, Dad.' She tried to concentrate on the unpromising group of letters in her hand, looking blearily at the board.

'I know I'm always accused of being slow,' her father, habitually a very thoughtful player, grinned, 'but that would be ridiculous. We always play Scrabble on Christmas Eve,' he explained to James. 'Gives the women,' here he winked, 'a chance to relax.'

'Relax!' His wife put down her word and picked up the last three tiles. 'No housewife ever relaxes till she's served the meal on Christmas Day. You men don't know the meaning of Christmas. Your turn, James.'

'Right.' He pondered for a moment before playing, then glanced across at his wife. 'You're tired, my sweet.' Jane made an ineffective attempt to disguise a yawn, at the same time wondering why that particular endearment was so invariably irritating—surely the two least sincere words in the vocabulary. He might even have chosen them for that very reason. She glared at him, then her expression softened as he turned to speak to her mother. 'Jane works such endless hours she's bound to be exhausted, especially after all the Christmas rush. Why don't you go up to bed when we finish this game?' He was looking at her again, so she had to adapt her expression. Bed? Had he mentioned bed, and what did he mean? She felt the breath being drawn from her body as they stared at each other, then her mother broke through the tension.

'Then,' with a flourish she put the last of her letters on the board, 'I'm finished. End of game.' She began to count up scores. 'Yes, do go up, Jane—you look weary, dear.' She added comfortingly, 'And remember, no special breakfast tomorrow, everyone fends for himself till lunchtime, so there's no need for you to be up early, darling. Would you like me to bring a drink upstairs for you?'

'Mum!' In a mood of affection Jane put her arm about her mother and held her close. 'You mustn't spoil me. I ought to be bringing things up to you, not the other way round. I promise I'll do that to-morrow. Oh, and in the morning I'll just have some coffee when I come downstairs, and after that we'll open our presents.' She tried to invest the words with some of the enthusiasm she usually felt for the event. 'Now I am feeling pretty tired, so I'll see you both in the morning. Goodnight, Mother, Father.'

'Goodnight, Jane.' Her father got up and crossed to a cabinet. 'I'm just going to let James sample some of that special whisky we brought back from Scotland last year. You needn't worry,' he set out two glasses and reached for the bottle, 'I promise you I shan't keep him too long.'

'I hope you'll stick to that, Alan. I know what you're like when you have someone to talk to, and you don't want to have a hangover in the morning.'

Fortunately, Jane thought as she lay in the wide double bed allowing fatigue to close over her, fortunately her mother's sensible admonition was being ignored, which saved her the trouble of pretending to be asleep. It...was...always so... unconvincing...'.

Somewhere in the dark hours of the night she moved, stretching out in bed, and her foot encountered another. It was pleasant enough to lie in the warm stillness, no longer quite asleep but not wholly awake either, to run her foot the length of a shinbone, to stay in some kind of contact.

Pleasant—more than that, the rub of skin against skin wakened a tingling sensation, one that made her murmur, stir a little, turn in the downy softness and throw out an arm. Something then reached out, moving gently, sensuously against the softness of her thigh. Again that...that disturbing... endlessly heady touch as the fine lawn of her nightdress rubbed against her, then the strength, the weight of a limb, an arm came across her as once it used to.

Another sound, deep and disturbed, from her own throat. Her lips parted and she turned, the thin material was pulled taut against her body, a hand suddenly demanding and possessive was brushing restraint aside, an arm underneath was raising her, fitting her against the flexed male body.

It was a dream, she wanted to believe it, and she prayed, quite feverishly she prayed it wouldn't end. So often she had imagined it, but always she was left unsatisfied, frustrated—though she shrank from the word.

Kisses feathered down over her closed eyelids, over the downy curve of her cheek, reaching her mouth, hesitating, finding no resistance but lips willing—no, much more than willing, eager to part, to abet the delicious onslaught, to aid the tumultuous exploration. The clean sweet scent of him was all about her, the taste of him on her tongue, his hands twisted in the looseness of her hair as if he meant to bind and keep her. Why, she wondered, why should he need to do that when all she wanted in the world, all she longed for was here, in these few feet of space, and now, when all she wanted to do was give...

'Jane,' his voice was coming to her from a great distance, 'I've so longed for you...' And before she knew it she was drifting off to sleep, more at peace than she had been for a very long time.

Waking was slow. She huddled beneath the duvet, unwilling to put her nose above the covers till, quite suddenly, struck by the most absurd thought, she sat bolt upright, and finding herself minus her nightdress, which more or less confirmed her wild ridiculous idea, she stared blankly at the slat of light coming through the curtains, then slid back under the covers. But still she could not resist running her palm the length of her body with slow recollective approval in the moment before she was stricken with the enormity of what she had allowed, what she had *encouraged* to happen.

How could you, Jane? How could you abandon your principles to such an extent, without even asking him about...oh, about all those things it was so vital for her to know. Why, James, didn't you tell me the Brazil job was for a married man instead of letting me find out by accident? Couldn't you have trusted me? It wasn't as if I was the one who was insisting on a wedding ring, that was your hang-up. And how was it that when I rang you one night it was Miranda who answered the telephone, it was she who fetched you from the bath. Oh yes, she did—I heard her myself calling you and... Oh, why hadn't she taken advantage of the moment's sweetness to find out? She would surely have forgiven him, but as it was, it was so humiliating. If she only knew, if she could be sure...

With one swift graceful move she rose from the bed. The sooner she was down there finding out, showing him that in spite of a momentary weakness there were questions to be answered. Quickly she showered and dressed, putting on the new dress, soft lambswool jersey in the most heavenly shade of hyacinth, figure-hugging in style, a narrow silver belt emphasising her trim waistline and... She brushed out her hair, pleased it looked so dark and bouncy, applied a light make-up and collected her carefully wrapped parcels from the cupboard.

Her heart was thumping wildly when she went downstairs, so it was a relief when James, just returned, so her mother informed her, from taking Joss for a run, didn't go overboard with his greetings, just the usual affectionate murmur, cheeks brushing against each other, a hand against her breast causing her to quiver.

'We've been dying for you to come down, Jane,' her mother's chatter was a welcome diversion, 'at least I have—you know what I'm like. I can never wait, and, besides, I'll be in the kitchen till lunchtime.'

'I'm planning to help you, Mother.' She was aware that James, standing slightly back, was watching her intently, and felt her skin grow hot. 'And these are my presents for you all.'

'This is gorgeous, darling!' Nancy drooled over the pink silk blouse. 'One of the perks of having a daughter working in fashion,' she explained to James. 'You come to look for such extravagant presents. And this lovely scent from you, James— you're both spoiling me, and I'm loving it.'

'And thanks for these.' Alan held up a recently published biography. 'I've been looking forward to reading this. And at the same time I'll sip your brandy, James. Total self-indulgence!'

'Thank you, darling.' James quietly approved the tapes of Russian choral music which Jane knew was one of his interests. 'And for the lovely brushes. I haven't seen any like these—it looks like mother-of-pearl.'

'Yes. They were discovered in one of the prop rooms—it seems they've been in an old cupboard since the thirties. It's hard to find anything of that quality nowadays. Along,' Jane hadn't meant to mention the subject, but it sort of slipped out, and in a sharp kind of way which fortunately only James seemed to notice, 'along with that bearskin coat.' It was a direct reminder of that night when things had started to go wrong between them and would have been better unsaid...

'Go on, then, Jane!' Her mother had been remarkably patient. 'I'm dying with curiosity about that exciting parcel from James!'

'All right.' Quickly, glad to be distracted from that long look he had given her, Jane took up the large flat package which had a smaller one dangling from the ribbons. 'It feels like a picture,' she smiled, determined to be natural even to the extent of smiling at James. 'Oh, yes, it *is*!' Arms extended, she held up the small oil-painting for them all to see. 'And I love it, James—thank you! Beautiful house, lots of trees around it, and who's the artist?' She frowned over the signature. 'Is it Abe something?'

'Abe Fisher. According to the chap who sold it to me, he was a pupil of a pupil of Palmer. If you can believe that...' James's smile and shrug indicated his own inclination.

'Don't mock him!' For a moment Jane forgot their situation and almost pouted at him, then she remembered, blushed and returned her attention to the landscape. 'I love the sheep grazing in the corner of the field there. I must find out about Palmer, I'm not very well up on these things. Mmm,' she rubbed a finger over the faded title plate, 'Barfleur House—unusual but rather nice.'

'Apparently this Abe Fisher had a great feeling for Normandy, spent much of his time there, but came back to England towards the end of his life. He bought this house and christened it after his favourite French port.'

'I wonder where it is?' Her father studied it. 'Any idea, James?'

'Not too far from here, in fact.' When Jane glanced up she was disconcerted by the expression in James's eyes. Slightly narrowed, they were watching her intently, and she had the feeling there was more to this than simply her reaction to a present. 'Just outside Amberley, in fact.'

'Interesting—but Jane, do open your other gift from James. Then I can go back to the kitchen with an easy mind. That little parcel is so intriguing.'

'My other...?' She was blushing again, conscious of James's eyes so firmly fixed on her, as she removed the gold paper from the tiny package. 'Earrings!' She took the exquisite wrought silver pieces from the box and held them up for inspection. 'So beautiful.' Her voice shook slightly, and she dared not look at James in case she burst into tears.

'Gosh, aren't they?' Nancy admired them. 'Tiny cages—they'll look gorgeous with that dress, Jane, do go and try them.'

Her fingers were so nervous that she could hardly hold them, but when they were fixed and she moved her head they all admired the way they turned and swayed, and the tiny jewels meant to portray caged exotic birds really gave that impression.

'Lovely!' Nancy sighed. 'I bet you bought them in Brazil, James.'

'I did. Special order.'

'You make me feel envious. I was so looking forward...'

'Well, if I go again, I promise you'll have the first invitation,' he told her.

'You think there's a chance of that?'

'Well, not in the immediate future.'

The way the conversation was going brought Jane right back to reality, and here was the chance to ask the question which had been stabbing at her

for days. 'And of course, Mother, you must remember that not all these positions are for married
men. The Brazil job was unusual in that respect—
isn't that so, darling?'

Maybe it was the endearment that took James
slightly by surprise, or perhaps it was more that he
didn't understand the drift of the question. In any
case, he could not for a second have imagined the
fearful anxiety with which she waited to hear his
answer. Would it clear her of the awful weight
resting on her shoulders, wipe away the suspicions
planted however unwittingly by Miranda, suspicions which she hoped and prayed would be proved
groundless? If last night had demonstrated nothing
else it had shown how much she needed him, wanted
them to be reconciled.

There was a hint of pleading in the shadowy brilliance of her green eyes. She wouldn't even mind
if he twisted the answer so that her acceptance could
be total. If she could spend the rest of the day—
Christmas Day, after all, she reminded herself in a
state of rising excitement—anticipating what would
happen when the door of their bedroom closed later
that night, and . . .

This time she would be ready for him, her arms
held out so that every slow movement in their love-
making would tease and delight. Her heart was
hammering loudly against her ribs. Lips parted, she
ran the tip of her tongue over them, prepared a
smile and . . .

'Of course it was for a married man.' His eyes were narrowed, puzzled, searching for some clue to her meaning. 'Otherwise I should hardly have been in a position to beg you to come out there, should I?' For all the good that did me, was implicit in the way he turned abruptly away, bending to touch the dog who had been demanding his attention.

For otherwise, Jane's beautiful green eyes were chips of ice as they gazed at his averted profile, otherwise you would never have thought of marrying me, would you? We could just have gone on and had the affair I suggested, we need never have gone through the charade of marriage, need never have made each other so miserable.

It was just as well her parents were still pottering about folding wrapping paper, repositioning Christmas cards, for she might easily have shouted the accusations at him instead of containing them inside her. Where they raged like a fever.

CHAPTER NINE

IN SPITE of an unusually bright mild January, Jane felt the winter to have been endless. Easy enough to identify that with the traumas of the Christmas season. First what had happened between her and James on Christmas Eve and then his precipitate departure the following day, something she might have been expected to regard with something approaching relief in the difficult circumstances but which turned out to be an additional burden. What she had wanted above everything was some kind of resolution of the conflict between them. She had hoped, in spite of everything, in spite of Miranda, in spite of his reasons for marrying, she had hoped the holiday extending over several days would provide the opportunity, but the telephone call just after lunch on Christmas Day put paid to that.

'I'm sorry, everyone,' he returned to the dining-room where they had been lingering over coffee until he was called to the phone, 'but I'm afraid I'll have to go.'

'Go? Oh, but you can't!' Nancy was obvious in her disappointment. 'Oh, James, no!'

' 'Fraid so, Nancy.' He glanced from her to his wife, who was gazing in disbelief and deep-down desolation. 'I'm really sorry.'

139

'But it's Christmas Day!' That fact was echoing in Jane's brain, excluding all other considerations. 'What,' she threw the question like an accusation, 'what can Atlantic want with *you*,' as her parents were still ignorant of the true situation it was as close as she dared come to mentioning it, 'today of all days?'

When he shrugged Jane could see he was frowning, his expression strained. 'I'm afraid oil wells aren't into Christmas. There's an emergency at one of our plants in Mexico and they want to try out some new equipment. I'm picking that up and flying out of Heathrow tonight.'

'What a pity.' Comfortingly Nancy covered her daughter's hand with her own. 'And just when you've been separated for such a long time. I'm so sorry...'

'Yes, damned bad luck, James. But at least they had the decency to wait till you'd had your Christmas dinner,' said Alan.

'Best I ever had.' The attempt at lightheartedness wasn't exactly successful; no one was in the mood. 'A car should be arriving in,' a quick glance at his watch 'oh, in about twenty minutes, so...' He returned his attention to his wife. 'Jane, this means you're left with the Jaguar. Think you can get it home for me?'

'I think I can manage.' She didn't feel the least bit like forgiving him. There was only so much she could cope with...

'Oh, you can trust her with your car, James. I'm sure she's told you she used to be keen on rallying at one time.' Alan was doing his best to reduce the tension he sensed between his daughter and her husband. 'She's one of the few women I'd trust with my own car.'

'Well, thank you, Alan.' Indignation mingled with amusement in his wife's voice. 'Now I know.'

'Joke, darling, joke. Besides, I did say one of the few. One of the two, I should have said, but don't ask the name of the other—I don't want you to become vain about your driving. Now, James, is there anything we can do?'

'I don't think so. I just have to grab a bag. Darling...' James appealed to his wife, 'you can take anything I have to leave behind.'

'Go and help him pack, Jane,' said Nancy. 'Your father and I will soon deal with the tidying up down here.'

Her own mother, thought Jane as she preceded her husband on the stairs—you'd think she would sense that the last thing she wanted right then was a tête-à-tête with her husband. She watched him walk purposefully about the room, retrieving shaving things from the bathroom, zipping up the leather grip and then standing looking down at her as she sat on the edge of the bed. He sighed. 'That's about it, I think. You can manage everything else?'

'I don't have much choice, do I? What I can't understand...

I thought your contract with that company was over.'

'Yes?' He gave a short bitter laugh. 'Is that what you thought? It isn't as simple...'

'I wouldn't have thought you'd be so long-suffering.' The instant Jane used the word she knew she had made an error. It was open to misinterpretation and...

'Nor would I.' His voice was hard, his expression confirming that he was choosing to relate her words to their personal situation, and additionally that he continued to blame her. 'Anyway,' he shrugged, sighing as she continued to look at him with raised eyebrows, 'I'm no more pleased than anyone else with what's happened, especially...' he turned away, crossed to the window and stood looking out '... when what we need more than anything else in the world is time to talk. We... can't go on like this.'

'I agree.' With an intense effort she was able to hang on to her control. A second's relaxation and she would have produced a wave of tears to engulf both of them. Feverishly she bit on her lower lip. '*I've* been waiting to talk since the day you got back from Brazil, but...'

'I know, I know, but things have been... well, hectic doesn't begin to touch what's been going on. But they're beginning to settle, and soon...'

'Soon...' Her voice very nearly broke, but she didn't imagine he'd notice. 'Soon it'll be too late.'

'It needn't be.' His voice had grown more tender, but that just made it more difficult for her. 'Not if we both want . . . Jane, what will you do? Will you wait down here with your parents? I don't want to think of you alone in that flat when . . .'

'I haven't decided. I might stick to the original plan and drive back tomorrow, before the worst of the rush starts.'

'That's my transport now.' James shrugged himself into the dark sports jacket, and looking up at him in the fading light Jane felt her heart turn over. This time tomorrow he would be at the other side of the world, she had no idea when she might see him again and . . . 'I'd better go. I should be back in a week or ten days.'

'A week?' She didn't think she could bear this uncertainty for another seven days. 'A *week*?'

'It's Mexico I'm going to,' amusement touched the impatience in his voice, 'not Brighton! Besides, I'm going out there to try to diagnose a problem, and they aren't always that easily solved.' He looked towards the door as he heard the loud summons on the knocker, then the sound of footsteps on the stair. 'Jane,' there was sudden urgency in his voice as well as a touching softness, 'about last night. I——'

'Forget,' although it was a whisper there was force behind it and a message in the fiery expression she turned on him, 'forget last night. It was a mistake, do you understand—a mistake!' And in spite of the gathering gloom she could have sworn that his face lost colour, and there was a long, awful silence.

'James,' there was a discreet knock at the door, 'your driver is here.'

'All right, Nancy, I'm just coming.' The silence was all about them while they continued to stare at each other, Jane all the time fighting her longing to raise a hand, to touch his in a gesture of—what? She couldn't quite explain. Tenderness, reconciliation, or maybe just regret that her tone had been so uncompromising, but in any case it was pointless, because the chance was gone, and he was speaking again.

'I hear what you're saying, Jane, but...' he sighed, bent to pick up his grip '...don't ask me to forget. I just can't do that.' Fleetingly she was aware of his lips brushing against her face. Still that urge to throw her arms about him, to hold him close, to refuse leave for him to go to Mexico, but he had gone before she had the chance to slip the rigid control which had been part of her for so long, before she could decide to let heart rule head. Only now there was nothing to hold her back. She could give way to the pain and misery of the last few months, find some relief in a paroxysm of weeping.

'It's such a shame, darling.' Later that evening she had to endure the well-meaning sympathy of her parents. 'I sometimes think these high-powered jobs make too many demands.' Her mother's tender pat on the shoulder was in fact a great comfort.

'Mmm.' Alan Wyatt took out his pipe and forgetful of his wife's dictum began to puff happily. 'On the other hand, flattering in a way. That young man driving the car—Clive, I think his name is—he said James is the only man in the company who can solve this particular problem.'

Which went to show . . . Jane excused herself and went into the kitchen where the half-devoured goose carcass lay with its garnish of red cabbage and parsnips. It only went to show—she began to stow away in cupboards the seldom used pieces of crockery—how very little your average chauffeur knows about the workings of a multi-national company.

She had not seen her husband since. The fact was a great source of offence, although she admitted it was not his fault entirely. The note he had left when he returned during her trip to Paris told her as much.

Jane, What's going on? I thought we'd agreed to talks! Please give me an early date when this will be possible. Contact me. I expect to be in Shetland for the next day or two. I give a number below where you can get in touch.

The note had been signed with a distinctive flourishing initial J, and she had been provoked into an equally steelly reply, saying she would be at home from now on as she had been for most of the past three months, and should he be so anxious to speak with her, etcetera, etcetera. The sheet of paper had been pinned prominently on a board in the kitchen, but as far as she could judge James had not been back at the flat, so he hadn't seen it.

In the meantime she had just about survived the January sales edition, even though it was much more hectic than she remembered from previous years, and now she was right in the middle of preparing the feature article she was expected to write about the summer collections which she had previewed in Paris.

'Lottie,' near the end of one particularly trying busy day, determined to catch up on some paperwork, she looked up with a groan, 'I don't suppose you have such a thing as an aspirin with you?'

'An aspirin?' Lottie frowned. 'What do you mean? Do you have a headache?'

'It's all right,' having rummaged for a few moments in a drawer, Jane produced a small bottle that rattled when she shook it, 'I've found mine here. Yes, I've had a rotten head since lunchtime, and...' With a weary sigh she pushed herself up from her desk. 'I'll just get some water. I hope these are still effective, they must have been in the drawer for ages...'

'Jane,' something in Lottie's tone arrested the younger woman, and she looked round, one eyebrow raised questioningly, 'do you think you should?' There was a moment's silence, then,

'Do I think I should what?' Jane frowned, bewildered.

'I mean...' Lottie was confused, something unique in Jane's experience '...all they say about drugs nowadays, and...things.' The expression in her eyes appeared to demand understanding. 'Side-effects, that kind of thing. Besides...' another peculiar hesitation '...I noticed you didn't drink your coffee first thing this morning.'

'No.' Jane was thoughtful as she recalled the effect the normally welcome drink had engendered. 'You're right, Lottie, I didn't. I left it too long, let it grow cold, and the sight of the film on top of the cup,' she shuddered delicately, smiling at herself as she did, 'it turned my stomach for a moment.' She frowned. 'Did you notice anything funny about it?'

'No, but I tell you what,' Lottie jumped up from behind her typewriter, 'I was speaking to Grace at lunchtime and she swears by camomile tea for headaches. I'll go and beg a sachet from her and you can test it.'

Jane returned to her figures, absently accepting the cup of straw-coloured liquid when it was set in front of her, sipping, then screwing up her face. 'Well,' she gave a tiny shiver, 'if the flavour's anything to go on this should do you good!'

'Nice, is it?'

'Vile is a more appropriate word, I think, but I suppose I'll have to give it a chance to perform. Now, Lottie, about this letter to Sheko Knits in Hong Kong, maybe we ought to give them another few days' grace if you think that's reasonable...'

It was late when at last they finished, and as they went down to the ground floor, Jane noticed how her colleague had been darting speculative glances in her direction. 'Come on, Lottie,' she smiled, 'I know you're dying to say something.'

'Me?' Lottie was amazed but somehow unconvincing. 'Well, I was simply wondering if your head is better.'

'Not too bad. Seven out of ten for the vile brew, shall we say?'

'That's something at least. I think herbal remedies are so much healthier, don't you?'

'I haven't given it much thought, to be honest.' Slightly puzzled by something in her companion's manner, Jane frowned. 'I'm not ill that often, so I don't take many pills and potions. I didn't know you were into alternative medicine either.'

'Any news of James?' Lottie went off on a tangent. 'Do you think he'll be back soon?'

They had reached the pavement and paused while Lottie put up her umbrella against the light rain. Jane waited till they were walking along the street before she replied, 'I don't *know* exactly, but I'm expecting him any time.'

'So it's nearly a month since you saw him.' Again there was the impression that Lottie wanted to say something, but she instantly hurried on. 'Well, when he does come back, tell him from me that he's to look after you. Goodnight.' And she hurried off in the direction of her bus stop.

Walking briskly towards her underground station, Jane allowed herself a little smile. Lottie was such a motherly soul, and had been looking after her since she had taken on the job as her assistant. Not only in the office either; she had been very protective as far as her private life was concerned, and Jane knew she would have been aghast if she had any idea of the true state of her marriage.

She had to stand on the way home. She tried to support herself by leaning against one of the upright posts, her newspaper folded carefully to reveal the crossword, though her brain was too clogged up for her to solve even one clue. Wearily she leaned her cheek against the cool metal. Although her head was better her stomach heaved as the train went into a bend at speed, and it was while she was trying to detach her mind from her slight nausea ... something in her brain clicked and began working overtime. Such an outrageous idea, just too crazy to contemplate, so wild that she felt her lips begin to curve in amused incredulity.

The train pulled in at her station, and, her mind busy with all kinds of mathematical tests, she walked rather slowly in the direction of the flat. It was strange, once the suspicion had been admitted it was hard to dislodge, and... Barely realising what she was doing, Jane stopped in front of a brightly lighted shop window, hesitated, debated, then walked inside and made a purchase.

Pregnant! Of course she didn't believe it. In spite of the evidence of the test. And she had heard there was a ten per cent margin of error. At least she thought so. Certainly she knew they weren't foolproof. She would wait another few days and do another test—simply to set her mind at rest, for she knew she wasn't. No—the shadowy eyes she raised to meet her own reflection in the mirror were frightened and unconvinced, and a moment later a wave of nausea took her dashing through to the bathroom—it just wasn't possible.

And by the time Sunday came round she was feeling so much better she decided to dismiss the fear from her mind. A leisurely breakfast of toast and coffee taken back to bed restored her confidence, and she hadn't had any more sickness. Most likely it was all down to her anxiety, and once things were settled . . . She got up, decided to take a walk in the nearby park, then come home with a pile of magazines and laze for the rest of the day. On her way she passed a chemist's shop, made the same purchase as before and achieved the same result.

Pregnant. As a result of that one incident on Christmas Eve. She didn't believe it could happen so easily. Especially it wouldn't happen to her. Long ago, long before she married, she had quite made up her mind that children, *if any*, would be carefully planned, times would be charted and selected, so all kinds of activities could be slotted in and . . . She was always so organised, that was one of the things she prided herself on, and now it was all to be swept away. Tears of self-pity and humiliation slid down her cheeks, and the only thing that came into her mind by way of distraction was the thought of a giant cream cheese sandwich topped with pickled gherkins and washed down with a huge cup of frothy cocoa.

The alarm on Monday morning made her groan as she struggled to sit up. Never, she assured herself, had the prospect of a day at Beaumont's held less appeal. It wasn't simply that she hadn't slept, that her mind had been whirling with massive problems, it wasn't that she had endured agonies of indigestion during the night, it was that she felt, probably for the first time in her life, utterly listless and apathetic about the world of high fashion and selling. If this was the effect pregnancy had on women then all her instincts had been right! She gave a deep sigh, allowed herself to close her eyes for ten seconds, then woke with a start to the knowledge that she had overslept.

A frantic rush, a choice of shower *or* breakfast, but with her stomach in its present state there was no contest. The quick make-up couldn't entirely hide the shadowy fatigue, the green eyes usually so vibrant with life had never looked so despondent, but, she thought as she reached for her handbag, Beaumont's would have to take her as she was, and if they had any objection...

She threw open the door of her bedroom, and her nostrils were at once assailed by... the smell of bread toasting, of coffee brewing and of bacon grilling, and as she paused James came out of the kitchen and stood there looking at her. He was wearing the dark trousers of a suit, a light shirt, and his maroon silk tie had been pulled down. Jane felt her heart gave the peculiar lurch signalling sheer joy and at the same time unparalleled dismay.

'Hi.' He took a step closer, his eyes searching her features intently. 'I got in about an hour ago.' His smile was quick and guarded. 'I thought...maybe we could start by having breakfast together.'

'Oh!' She felt like bursting into tears, or throwing herself into his arms, or something equally inappropriate.

'Oh, yes—and,' he turned, picking up the sheet of paper she had left for him in the kitchen, 'I got your message.'

'Ah!' Remembering how sharp she had been, how bitter, Jane felt herself grow quite cold.

'Now what do you say? Is it breakfast,' he was setting out to charm and entice as he had that first morning in the Ocean Bay—if only the response could be as easy, as direct and uninhibited!—'or pistols for two?'

And clammy. There was a distinctly clammy feel to the palms of her hands. And giddy. She tried to concentrate on his face, but it swam about in front of her eyes, so she reached for the hall table and held on. The picture steadied.

'I've grilled a pile of bacon just as you like it,' he went on persuasively. 'Do you think you can manage two eggs?' He was in the act of turning back into the kitchen when the enormity of his suggestion hit her with the force of a tidal wave.

He should *know* she loathed the thought of bacon, the smell was enough to make her heave, and... She dropped her handbag on the floor, put a desperate hand to her mouth and simply flew through her bedroom and to the bathroom, pushing ineffectively at the door before she started retching over the basin.

Until she had finished she didn't know, or much care, if James was there, but as she raised her head, reaching for a tissue to wipe her eyes, she saw his reflection behind her in the mirror. His dark eyes were full of concern, as he came closer, putting his arms round her, holding her, patting her back comfortingly. She was aware of his chin resting on the top of her head for a delicious moment before he drew back to look down into her face. 'Jane, what's the matter? Have you been ill?'

She shook her head. 'Of course not.' No matter how wonderful it would be to stay there, to lean against him feeling his strength support her, she couldn't. As it was she was bound to be horribly late and...a rep was coming to see her at ten... She tried to smile. 'You know me, I'm never ill.' Firmly she detached herself, checked her appearance and reached for her toothbrush.

'You don't look well. I thought so the moment I saw you.'

It was the last thing she wanted to hear. She rinsed her mouth, replacing the glass with an angry little clink. 'I've had a worrying few months. *That* probably explains my altered looks.' The accusation in her reply ought to have been satisfying, but instead she felt the sting of tears as she went to brush past him. 'I'm going to be late.' But he caught her arm and swung her, none too gently, round to face him.

'That wasn't what I meant. I...'

But that unexpected swinging move was the last straw for Jane that morning. The floor began to weave in an alarming way beneath her feet, the flowers on the carpet came up to surround her and she was falling down a deep chasm.

When she came to a moment later, she was lying on the bed, the duvet had been thrown over her and the loud noise in her ears materialised into the frantic voice of her husband having some kind of argument with a doctor's receptionist. 'Well, the moment you *can*, contact Dr Fairfax ask him to ring me. It's extremely urgent, my wife is ill and... Yes, I do understand, but...well, if I don't hear something in the next few minutes I shall have to... Yes, flat number 24—he knows where to come. Thank you.'

With a weary little smile Jane turned her face into the pillow, longing for nothing more than the chance to go to sleep for a long time, but when she heard footsteps she began to sit up. 'James,' she held out a hand, 'there's no need...'

'Jane!' The note of desperation struck her to the heart. 'Jane!' He held her hand cradled for a moment against his cheek, then dropped a kiss against the palm. 'Roddy Fairfax is caught up in a traffic jam, but he'll be here as soon as he can move. How are you feeling now?'

'Tired.' The great lump that had been lodged in her chest was easing. 'But I'm perfectly all right.'

'Are you?' He sounded doubtful, his dark eyes raking her features as if determined to penetrate the recesses of her mind.

'Yes, and I must get up and go to the office, even if I am going to be hours late.' She started to sweep aside the covers, until he stopped her.

'There's no way you're going till we've seen the doctor. I've just been waiting,' he glanced at his watch, 'till I thought Lottie would be at her desk, and I'm going right away to tell them you won't be in . . .' He got to his feet.

'But I must . . .'

'Tell me,' he was sounding the least bit exasperated and as dominating as he had ever been, leaning forward to replace the duvet, 'when was the last time you had any sick leave?'

'Oh, a long time. The winter before last I had two days off with flu, and . . .' The prospect of a day in bed was pretty well irresistible, and since it wasn't her decision . . .

He was back in a few minutes. 'Seems to be all right. In fact, I got the idea Lottie wasn't very surprised. She's given me a list of instructions. I'll just give Roddy another two minutes . . .' He looked worriedly at his watch.

'James,' now it was Jane's turn to show exasperation, 'please will you listen? There's really no need to be so concerned, there's nothing Roddy can do...'

'Jane?' His voice was anguished and it was a split second before she realised what kind of impression she might have given.

'James,' she ignored the brief giddiness as she sat up, 'I promise you it's nothing serious. It's just... I'm going to have a baby.'

'A baby?' For a moment she thought he hadn't understood, then the agony disappeared from his expression, to be replaced by one she couldn't identify. 'My God!' He sank on to the chair beside the bed, raked his hands through his hair and then looked at her. 'Jane! I'm so...so desperately sorry.'

That was when she could no longer suppress the tears.

CHAPTER TEN

IT WAS blissful to lie comfortably in the warm bed. Outside Jane could hear the occasional sound of a car engine, the wind sighing among the tall buildings and an occasional splatter as rain hit the windowpanes. And the greatest pleasure of all was knowing that somewhere close at hand James was moving quietly about the flat. Jane felt that after carrying a heavy load alone for a long time, she had been able to hand it on to someone else, someone much more capable of bearing it and who would at the same time protect and care for her.

Roddy Fairfax had called, confirmed her diagnosis, assured her that she was 'just fine' and 'blooming' in a matter-of-fact kind of way, then had breezed out of her bedroom after telling her to pop round to his consulting-rooms as soon as possible. Then she was aware of a lengthy doorstep discussion in which the words 'scrum' and 'pack' and 'try' were frequently used, before James came back into the room. He shrugged his shoulders and smiled apologetically.

'He's still rugby-mad, I'm afraid, has been since we were at school together, and of course he did play for England one year. He was just as casual when his own wife had children, so I imagine on the whole he thinks rugger is the more interesting topic! Anyway,' he came forward, sat on the bed, put up a hand to brush a strand of hair back from her forehead, his face serious now, concerned, and he sighed as if he might have been clinging on to a slender thread of hope, 'that's that.'

Jane nodded, much too emotional to speak, and bit fiercely on her lower lip.

'Try not to worry, Jane. It'll all work out—you'll see. Now, I tell you what, you must be hungry—are you?' Another nod, the beginnings of a watery smile. 'Why don't I go and fix you something to eat? Did I get it right...you don't feel like eating a cooked breakfast?'

'You could say that,' she agreed.

'Then can I recommend the toast and coffee?'

'Not coffee.' Just the thought of her favourite beverage made her feel queasy. 'But tea and a slice of toast.' Something in his expression, warm and tender, brought some pink to her cheeks. 'That would be heavenly.'

It tasted that way too, helped by one of their best linen place-mats and a napkin, freshly squeezed orange and carefully browned pieces of toast. 'Come on, sit up.' James put a hand behind her, apparently quite detached, which quite definitely she was not. She caught her breath as his hand brushed her bare shoulder, resting for an instant in the small of her back. 'Sorry,' he was turning the situation into a joke, 'I ought to have had a rose at hand for your tray, to tempt you. Now, when you finish this, you're going to lie down and go to sleep. I shall be here all the time, so you needn't worry about a thing.'

It was much the same at lunchtime. He managed to produce some delicious consommé with Melba toast, a small portion of yoghurt and a perfect ripe peach.

'How on earth...?' Jane indicated the quite lavish meal. 'I don't as a rule have anything half as substantial!'

'Don't ask how I did it.' He grinned. 'Maybe I've been busy in the kitchen all morning. Just eat it, that's all I ask.'

She smiled to herself when he had gone, fairly certain he had been in touch with their local delicatessen who were always happy to deliver, and rather to her own surprise she was able to eat everything he had left. And then it was all too easy to slip down in the bed and to drowse away the rest of the afternoon. She felt not a trace of guilt at such self-indulgence, more relief that she found herself, even for a few hours, divorced from all the stir and bustle of her normal life.

But by late afternoon she knew she was thoroughly rested and had no inclination to lie a moment longer. She got up then, filled the bath, threw in a generous measure of her favourite bath oil and lay in the warm water with just a brief thought for all that might be going on at Beaumont's at that time of day. None of it seemed to matter, that was what was so strange.

A pair of dark flowery harem pants chosen for their extreme comfort, a short loose top in a colour close to jade. She brushed out her hair, applied a light make-up and then, conscious of her heart fairly hammering against her ribs, she left her bedroom.

James was in the sitting-room where she had expected him to be, but unusually appeared to be reading a paperback novel. It was so long since she had seen him with anything other than a pile of computer data in his hand that she stared. He rose when she opened the door and came towards her, and they stood looking at each other, then his hand touched her elbow in a protective gesture. 'Darling,' even if the word slipped out unguardedly it still caused a throb in the pit of her stomach. 'How are you feeling now?'

'I feel absolutely fine.' With the truth she surprised herself. It was so long since she could have given that answer honestly. Wide-eyed, she looked at him, searching his face for some clue as to his feelings, his thoughts. But she found herself instead beguiled by the sheer magnetism of the man she had married. How was it she had tried to go on without him for long? She couldn't face . . . But just now it was . . . well, it was like a dream to have him treat her like some very precious commodity, helping her to a seat at one end of the sofa, then perching on a stool in front, looking at her with such close attention and . . .

'Truly?' He leaned back, hands linked about his raised knee. He sounded doubtful, and it was a moment before she remembered what they were discussing.

'Truly,' she laughed, throwing back her head, though keeping her eyes fixed on his, knowing she would never get tired of doing just that. 'Truly, James, I feel fine. I think...' suddenly her eyes were brilliant with tears, 'I'm sure it was just that I felt so tired. I told you, I haven't been sleeping well.'

'And how long...' he reached out to her hand, a brief, almost an apologetic touch ' ... how long have you had this... this other worry on your mind?'

'Just:... just a few days. It was... it was Lottie.' Her tiny giggle, her sudden lightheartedness surprised her. 'She first made me think, nudged me in the right direction.'

'Mmm,' he said reflectively. 'I thought there was something about the way she spoke, not smug exactly but... knowing. I can see that now.'

'I suppose,' feeling her skin grow warm, Jane flicked her eyes away and back again, 'when she saw that I couldn't drink my morning coffee, usually my lifeline, she put two and two together and came up with the right answer before anyone else.'

'Indispensable Lottie!' James was watching her closely. 'But now we have to discuss things. I want you to tell me exactly how you feel. I know how much of a blow it must be, not at all what you hoped or planned,' he gave a sigh and looked away from her. 'The problem is...' He got up, walked to the window and stood looking down into the darkened gardens before returning to lean against the mantelpiece. He was frowning, the splayed-out fingers of his right hand under his chin. 'What are we going to do about it?'

'What...' Her heart gave a feverish leap, and she lay back against the cushions, suddenly bone-weary and just a little frightened. 'Wh—what do you mean?'

'Don't look at me like that, Jane.' There was the beginning of a smile on his face. 'Don't look so nervous.' He half turned, gazing down into the leaping flames of the fire. 'What I ought to have said was, what do *you* want to do?'

Instinctively, she had no idea she was reacting to some hidden threat. Her hand went to her lower abdomen, and she felt an unexpected melting tenderness for the tiny blob which would turn soon into a recognisable human being. Her child, it was, hers and James's. She reached hastily for her handkerchief, grateful that with his averted profile James was unlikely to notice, and then, because of her struggle for self-control, her voice had a hard cool edge when at last she could find a few words. 'In the circumstances I shall just have to cope, shan't I? As you say, it wasn't planned, but since it's happened... Certainly,' she burst out with indignation, 'I'd never dream...'

'Of what?' Now his frown had deepened, he was looking directly at her, then after a moment's fraught silence he gave a short bitter laugh. 'That? My God, it never crossed my mind. Do you imagine for a moment I'd allow you to take such a risk? And——'

'From what I've been told,' she spoke wearily, scarcely considering her words, 'there's very little risk these days. Certainly less than having a baby...'

'Ah,' his expression was bleak, 'then in that case I plead guilty to putting you at risk.' Ignoring her attempt to protest, he went on, 'And if there were some means of undoing it...'

'I'm not blaming you, for heaven's sake!' The words burst from her lips, and she meant them; she who had been blaming him for one thing and another over the past months was now released from the awful burden. 'James, we were both responsible—you didn't force me, and I refuse to use the word blame. I'm going to have a baby, it was totally unplanned, unforgivable in this time and place, but there, it's a fact, and I'm...' She felt a moment's qualm as for a split second she considered how it was going to affect her career at Beaumont's. 'I'm going to try to make the best of it.' This was another first, her acceptance that life was about to change, from the comfortable financial affluence provided by two generous salaries, and now... A tiny shiver as the economic realities were recognised, but she thrust from her mind the realisation that with neither of them earning . . .

'I blame myself entirely.' James raked his fingers through his dark hair. With a quiver of tenderness Jane noticed it was a shade longer than usual. He had always been so particular about a certain length, but he had been so busy, so involved, so many things on his mind. 'I should never have rushed you into marriage as I did.' His words were like a douche of cold water, and for a long time she sat there staring up at him, unable to find words to answer, but he went on. 'God knows why I didn't seize your offer.' A tiny shrug, a smile that accorded badly with the look of strain on his face. 'That way—well, at least you would have been a free agent, not tied down to a male chauvinist.'

'But . . .' She wanted to deny that he was what he claimed, to insist that she had been wilful and selfish, but there was something to be cleared up before they went any further. 'But it wouldn't have been any good, would it?' Her voice grew more passionate. 'It would have been no good for the job in Brazil. Oh, James, I can't tell you how sorry I am—if it hadn't been for me . . .'

He passed a hand across his forehead as if in an attempt to clear his mind. 'I'm a bit off net, I'm afraid, Jane. I just can't understand . . . *What* was it you said about the job in Brazil? I simply can't see . . .'

'Miranda told me,' she smothered a tiny sob, 'and when I asked you confirmed it. The job in Brazil was for a married man, and...'

'That's right, no secret about it.' He showed no sign that her words had clarified anything for him, rather the reverse. 'So...'

'Well...' She shrugged, as if a show of indifference could begin to ease the pain. 'If you'd told me why you were so keen to be married, we might have discussed it, I could have explained how I felt, we could have decided together——' She continued even as he tried to interrupt, 'It could have saved us both a great deal of...' she changed her mind about using the word heartbreak '...a lot of worry.'

'Jane!' He moved then, coming towards her, teeth gleaming, and shook his head in mild reproof, put up a hand and trailed it down her cheek, a gesture that unfailingly caused a shiver in the region of her spine. 'Jane,' his tongue lingered over her name, 'where do you pick up such crazy ideas? Because it was a position for a married man there's no law that says you *have* to be married!' He laughed softly, intimately. 'I would still have gone there if we'd never met.'

'Oh!' Now that he had explained it was hard to understand why that hadn't always been perfectly obvious. 'Oh, I see...'

'And here you were thinking...did you really think I married you so I'd qualify for some job or other?'

'No, not really.' Her mind was now refusing to be honest.

'I've always thought…' He came closer, touched her cheek again with one finger, oblivious, or so it would appear, to the effect this might have on her. 'I thought you'd never have the slightest doubt as to why I married you.' Colour flooded into her face and her pulses were bounding in agitation. 'Now, maybe we ought to leave the subject for the time being, think about everything. It's all much too important to be rushed. I think——' It was a moment before he went on; she felt maybe he was waiting for her to say something, but while she was struggling to find the right words to describe what she had been through over the last months he changed the subject completely. 'You must be feeling hungry. What do you say to an omelette with salad? There's some french bread and a special fruit salad to follow.'

'Sounds perfect.' She settled into the corner of the settee. 'Would you like any help in the kitchen?'

'If you even think of moving from that seat . . . !'

'It's all right.' She laughed, and raised her hands in surrender. 'I shan't argue about it. Besides,' lowering her eyes, she looked down at her hands, 'I'm very impressed—so much cooking!'

'Mmm,' he sighed wearily, 'I'm worn out with it, but, since it appears I've no choice, back to the grind.' He got up and strolled to the door. 'And when you've eaten, I'm going to insist you go back to bed and rest. Roddy did say you were to take it easy for a day or...'

'Did he?' Jane lay back, her eyes openly challenging. 'I had the impression he was much more interested in last Saturday's rugby than...'

'Well, that too, of course,' he laughed. 'I did explain that the man is fanatical about the game, but he did just remember to mention his patient when I jogged his memory. Anyway, I was going to suggest, if you feel up to it, that is, you might like to come along on a drive tomorrow.'

'I'm not an invalid, James, and by rights I ought to have gone in to work today. But since you seem to have arranged some sick leave then there's no reason why...'

'It will depend on how you feel.'

She sighed. 'It's very nice to be treated like an invalid for a little while, but...'

'All right, all right!' There was a gleam in his dark eyes as they held hers and she could see all the warm topaz glints in the light from the leaping flames. 'I'll make a note of that. Oh...' About to go through the door, he paused. 'I see you've got the Abe Fisher hanging on the wall in your bedroom.'

'Yes.' No point in telling him that she had hung it there so she could see it first thing in the morning, last thing at night; through the days and weeks it had seemed the only fragile thread of contact between them. 'Yes, the more I look at it, the more

I like it. Thank you for giving me such a lovely present, James.'

'Good,' he said with what she thought was an excessive degree of satisfaction, and went out, closing the door softly behind him, leaving her alone in the room he had brought her to when they came back from the Caribbean. He had—she recalled it now with an achy little pain in her chest— he had swept her up in his arms, elbowing doors aside and then whirling her round before they both collapsed semi-hysterically on to the settee.

And there they had lain for a time, the laughter slowly slipping away from them as they gazed at each other. Her hands, at first linked loosely about his neck, had twisted in his hair, and she was guiding his mouth down to hers. And holding him, holding him.

Remembering, her eyes glazed, Jane stared into the flickering flames. If only... if only one could stay at that pitch of happiness for ever. At one time she had thought *they* would, it had been so very special, so unique, and she wanted, more than anything in the world she wanted to regain something of that relationship.

But deep inside her there was uncertainty, a tiny fragment of what James had said a little while ago was nagging at the back of her mind, then she remembered with a stab of anguish. 'I should never have rushed you into marriage.' The words echoed through her brain and no amount of reasoning would chase them away. She was sure, painfully sure, they were the ones James had used.

CHAPTER ELEVEN

TO SAY that Jane was dismayed, in spite of all James's tender solicitude, at sleeping on her own still would have been an understatement. Even if they hadn't made love, the joy of lying against him, the closeness of the marriage bed, would have been enough. To reach out in the night, to murmur his name, to touch, seemed like bliss. Except—she allowed herself a tiny smile—look where that circumstance had landed them. Lying in the darkness, she placed the palm of her hand wonderingly against her stomach. And she was asleep in five minutes.

She was emerging in the morning from a comfortable drowse when James appeared at her bedside with a cup of tea, and when he enquired she was able to assure him with total frankness that she was feeling perfectly fit.

'Mmm.' As she sat up, pushing the tumble of hair back from her forehead, he studied her. 'I wonder if that was the source of the trouble.'

'What do you mean?' Aware that the strap of her nightdress was slipping from her shoulder, Jane made no move to fix it, but while reaching out to the bedside table for her cup she was careful to flick a quick glance to check his reaction.

'I mean,' he was slow in replying, 'you've always been one to rush like a whirlwind in the morning. Perhaps if you were to take things more slowly...' As he turned away she tried to ignore her disappointment. After all, it was irrational to expect... Just because *her* heart was threatening to go into orbit it didn't mean... She raised the cup and drank thirstily.

'Delicious tea, James, just how I like it.' Anything to detain him for a few more seconds.

'Mmm.' There was something decidedly strange, almost defensive in his manner. He was holding on to the door as if it were a shield. Jane knew her own breathing was rapid and shallow, she suspected her eyes had a dreamy expression, and it was as if she were recognising for the first time something she had always known, that she was married to the most wonderful man. Even in the faded jeans, the comfortable open-necked shirt, he looked...well, certainly there was nothing the least bit ordinary about him. She understood he was waiting for an answer to some question, and blinked. 'I'm sorry, what did you say?'

'I said,' the dry note in his voice sent a tingle up her spine, 'you're on no account to move from that bed until I've brought your breakfast.'

'All right.'

'Then, and only then, shall we decide if you're well enough to come down to Sussex with me. At least the weather doesn't seem too bad; they're promising us some sun later.'

'Very well, James.' She was all wifely meekness, and she knew from the glint in his eye that he was as amused at this unusual facet of her character as she was herself. After that he closed the door quite rapidly, and she was left with nothing to do but eye herself in the mirror of the dressing-table opposite and wonder just why she had put on this particular nightdress. The top was figure-hugging lace, cut very low and leaving not a great deal to the imagination. She couldn't *quite* admit that she had seduction in mind... temptation, maybe, but seduction...?

It was ten o'clock before James allowed her to put a foot on the floor, another hour before she had showered and dressed. Again for no particular reason she had decided to wear the green silk blouse she had worn on the flight out to the West Indies, the blouse that made her eyes seem more intensely green, but a moment's consideration and she rejected the suede mini-skirt—much too flighty for an expectant mother, to say nothing of the time of year. Instead she chose a warm brown wool skirt, calf-length with a matching serape which looked practical and trendy when worn with polished brown boots. She didn't—she checked her appearance in the mirror—think she was letting the world of high fashion down.

Another smear of blusher, as she looked a little pale, a touch of pinky brown lipstick; she decided against eye make-up but smoothed her dark arched eyebrows with a damp finger, and that was about

all, except . . . Her hands shook slightly as she fixed
in her ears the delicately wrought silver cages James
had given her for Christmas.

'Comfortable?' They had been driving for almost
an hour, and she had begun to feel drowsy again
when he spoke, with that gentle dreamy music all
about them and the heat and everything.

'Oh, yes, perfectly comfortable.' Her original fear
that she might spoil their day by feeling sick had
been completely forgotten.

'Shouldn't be much longer.'

'Oh? Right.' She had no idea where they were
going or why, but it came to her that maybe their
outing was concerned with his search for a job, and
if so, doubtless it would be a relief to him if she
were to entertain herself for a bit. 'If you want to
drop me off anywhere, James.'

'Drop you off?' He swung off the main road,
slowed as they turned again and began to travel
along a winding country lane. 'No, there's no need
for that. Why do you think I brought you here?'
About him was an air of contained excitement
which made her look at him questioningly.

'I've really no idea.'

'You'll soon find out.' He turned and grinned,
so naturally, so disturbingly like the man she had
married that her heart simply flipped over inside
her chest. A moment later the car slid into lower
gear as he turned in between stone gateposts, over-
grown with green and yellow ivy, along a drive lined
with mature trees. It was easy to imagine how this

place would look in spring, all green and verdant with overhead a canopy of leaves, very English with the meadows at either side. The one on the left, Jane was sure, would go down to a splashy stream with buttercups and——

'Here we are!' Quite suddenly they emerged from a little copse which sheltered a group of buildings and pulled up on an apron of gravel in front of a house.

'James——' Her hand reached for the release button of her safety-belt and she was scanning the features of the house. It was so familiar, and yet... elusively different. 'James,' her voice grew more excited as it came to her all at once, 'it's Barfleur House! How clever of you to find it!' She got out and threw the end of her serape over her shoulder, leaned on top of the car, surveying the place through narrowed eyes. 'It's larger than I thought, and...yes, there's an extra window above the front door. And some of the trees are different.'

'Mmm—well, it's more than a hundred years since your picture was painted, so it's bound to have altered.' James grinned, jangling some keys in front of her eyes. 'I expect you're dying to see inside.'

'How on earth did you manage all this?' she demanded.

'Ah.' The front door swung back and they were in a nicely shaped hall. The floor was of polished oak with one or two rugs and the staircase wound up to a galleried landing. 'I'll tell you all about that later.'

'Lovely kitchen,' she approved the gleaming red Aga and other modern amenities which had been achieved without detracting from the period atmosphere. She loved the views from the three large rooms downstairs and upstairs, two delightful bathrooms rich with the dark Victorian mahogany and brass fittings, four large bedrooms and one smaller room, the only one unfurnished. 'It's just so lovely—people would go mad about the bathrooms. But who does it belong to, James?' They were in the main bedroom, Jane standing at the window enjoying the view, deciding she had been right about the stream; there was a gleam of water to her right. 'Who would let strangers have the run of their house—so much lovely furniture too, and they've even left the heating on for us? James?' When there was no answer she swung round. He was looking at her with a strange expression. 'I was asking,' she took a step closer, 'whose . . .'

'It's yours.' His voice was low, even a little husky. 'If you'll have it, Jane, the house is yours.'

'James!' A small chair, upholstered in a material which took up one of the colours in the curtains and bedcover, was at her hand, and she sank into it, her mind totally confused by the words she thought she had heard. 'Wh—what did you say?'

'You asked me who the house belonged to, and I'm saying it's yours. Ours. If I can persuade you to come and live in it.'

'Persuade?' Her tone was uneven, and she shook her head as if she would force understanding. 'I still don't know...'

'Jane,' he had come closer, sitting on the arm of her chair and taking her hand in his, 'I've always loved this place. It belongs to a friend, but he's been abroad for a long time. He always meant to come back here to live, but now he's met someone in Australia and they've decided to settle there. He always promised me first chance to buy should he decide to sell, and——'

'But...' There was so much to be considered. He was out of a job, she was having a baby and... Panic threatened to overwhelm her. Hadn't he said he ought not to have married? 'You mustn't James! It's too much...it isn't necessary, and besides...' the eyes she raised to his were brilliant with unshed tears '...you did say...' Unwilling to let him see her naked emotions, she looked swiftly down at their linked fingers and *defied* the tears to fall.

'Besides...' he prompted, his voice very gentle, so gentle that she felt a tear drop on to the back of her hand.

'Besides, you said you shouldn't have married me.' The pain of that implication stuck at her like a dagger. 'Anyway,' she gnawed feverishly at her lower lip, 'this is a house for a family.'

'Which,' his fingers brushed away the sprinkle of tears, 'which is exactly what we seem to have started.' Releasing his hand from hers, he put it under her chin, forcing her head upwards. For as

long as she could she kept her eyes averted, then
when she conceded he was smiling at her, shaking
his head reprovingly. 'And as for my views on our
marriage, where did you get such a crazy idea?'

'From you.' Her mouth trembled. 'That's what
you said yesterday.'

'A very cunningly edited version, if I may say
so. What I said, certainly what I meant was, I
shouldn't have married you as I did. It was unfair
to rush you. And selfish. I wanted you so much,
and I was afraid if I gave you time to think...'

In an instant she was deliriously, madly happy,
so blissful that for a moment she couldn't think
what had happened. 'Oh, James!' She reached up
and touched his face, slightly hesitant but de-
lighting in the firm touch of his skin. 'You mustn't
say that!' Her fingers reached his mouth and she
held them there, stifling any denial he might make.
'I was in just as much of a rush as you,' remembering that fact brought a wave of colour to her
cheeks, 'at least as much!'

At that he laughed, a deep throaty, chuckle which
had her lips curving in sympathy. 'Yes,' he admitted, 'I do remember. But I should have slowed
the pace. I was more experienced than you and
should have given you more time. Now,' he sighed,
though he didn't look unduly downcast, 'I feel I've
deprived you of something precious, something
important to women—the slow delicate business of
courtship, of getting to know each other. I wish I
hadn't taken that from you. And now...'

'James,' she held his hand against her cheek, 'you gave me exactly what I wanted. Don't blame yourself for anything—I wouldn't change things.'

'Now,' gently he pulled her to her feet, held her against him, 'I'm trying to make amends. I'm determined not to rush you, to give you time and space if you need it. When all the time my instinct is to...' He held her at arm's length then, smiling ruefully. 'Well, I'd better not go into that! In fact, if I'm to have any chance of sticking to my decision, I think we'd better leave this room. There's all the outside to see. I think you'll like the gardens, and...' Reluctantly Jane followed him from the bedroom, but when she saw the spacious outbuildings she was interested in his plans for converting a part into a flat should they decide they needed help with the house and grounds.

'What I don't understand, James——' They had returned to the kitchen and he was busy with the hamper of food he had produced from the boot of the car. He looked up when her voice died away.

'Yes?' He unpacked two glasses and set them on the table. 'What don't you understand?' Swiftly he pulled a cork, poured some wine and handed a glass to her.

'What I don't understand is...' Swirling the golden liquid, Jane stared down for a moment, then touched it to her lips. 'How is it you can afford a place like this when you're out of a job? Oh, James,' quite suddenly, surprising even herself, she had this urge to tell him what she had planned, 'I thought I'd be able to keep us both for a while. Just till you found another job, you understand? But I don't think,' intense disappointment made her screw up her eyes for a moment, 'at least ... I know my salary at Beaumont's won't go anywhere near paying the mortgage on a house like this. I did so want to do it, to try to make up to you, and of course,' she shrugged, struggling to regain her control, 'now with a baby coming ... I'm not sure what my position with the company will be.'

'Jane,' James sipped a little wine, frowned and then sat down close to her, 'forget about Beaumont's for the moment.' His eyes, she noticed, were very clear, and possibly because he was facing the window the amber flecks were obvious. 'The real question, now you've had the time to think of it, is what do *you* think about having the baby? I know it isn't what you wanted, but as it's happened, what do you feel about it?'

Her answer when it came was slightly dreamy, certainly reflective, not like Jane Barnard, senior fashion editor, at all. 'Strangely, and I never thought I'd ever hear myself say this but I feel rather ... excited. Certainly I don't want to change things now.' An apologetic smile curved her mouth as she turned to look at him. 'Is this really me talking? I ask myself.'

'My love!' He took her hand from the table, held it for a moment, then sighed. 'And bless you for everything you just said. Now, I'd better come clean. The redundancy from Atlantic was just a technicality. The whole company was being re-organised, certain positions were merged and rationalised, and when I knew what was going on, I moved heaven and earth to get back to London. And to you.'

'James . . .' It was a broken little murmur. She wondered if she would ever be able to tell him how sorry she was.

'I was so bitter at the time.' He shrugged, and though there was a smile too he couldn't entirely conceal his sense of hurt. 'I couldn't believe you'd refused to go with me. Even when I was out there I kept expecting you to arrive from the airport. And then, when I got back that first night and you said you were going out with Arthur Davis, I was so angry . . .'

'You can't have been jealous!' she exclaimed.

'Can't I indeed? I promise you I can quite easily. It's something I never experienced until I met you, and even though I knew I was being totally ir-rational it made no difference . . .'

'Just as I was jealous of Miranda.'

'Miranda?' he frowned. 'Why Miranda?'

'I rang you one night. I was so desolate without you I felt I couldn't go on another minute, but it was Miranda who answered the telephone. "He ees in the shower," ' she tried not very successfully to mimic the sultry accent, ' "I weel get heem for you." It would have been strange if I hadn't been jealous.' Remembering the violence of her reaction, she couldn't entirely control the tremor in her voice. 'And I was—wildly, madly jealous!'

James stared at her, a tiny frown pulling his eyebrows together, then he appeared to remember. 'Ah, so that was you? Yes, Miranda did come and yell outside the bathroom door. She'd called round to the flat to pick up some papers—and,' he grinned suddenly, his eyes sparkling mischievously, 'purely as a matter of interest, she had her eight-year-old grandson with her.'

'Her...' It was too much to cope with, her brain couldn't adjust so easily. 'I didn't even know she was married.'

'She isn't—never has been. But that has little bearing on the fact of her grandson. Also, it seems the right time to emphasise, though Miranda and I are good friends and I value her efficiency in the office, I've never felt that way about her, nor I suppose has she for me. For as long as I've known her she's been having an affair with one of Brazil's leading politicians. So you see, the lack of romantic interest is mutual.'

'Really?' Well, Jane had her own opinion about that, but certainly now that she was reassured about his position she didn't want to think about Miranda, and, besides, there was this other thing to be considered. 'And... you're still with Atlantic Oil?'

'I'm afraid so.' He took her hand again, dropped a kiss on the palm. 'I'm now Technical Director, Northern Europe. It's a big job, so you need have no worries about the house; we can afford it quite easily. Can you forgive me for being so devious? Truly I hadn't planned it that way, but it came into my mind the day I came home, then it was difficult to get out of it. I imagine I was playing for your sympathy.'

'Certainly you succeeded in making me feel guilty. Maybe that was what you wanted.'

'I can't believe it,' he considered. 'On the other hand... But tell me, did it work?'

'Of course it did, you wretch. I was tortured by the idea that my pigheadedness might have cost you your job.'

'So you admit, you are pigheaded.'

'Wilful, pigheaded, ambitious and——'

'Ssh!' James put a finger to her lips. 'You're speaking of the woman I adore, the mother of my children and...'

'Child,' Jane interrupted quite sharply.

'Well, I'm happy to start with one, but... you did mention ambition. That's something you've never hidden from me, and I'm concerned about how you feel. You've never pretended your career wasn't important.'

'Well,' Jane spoke slowly, as if for the first time she herself was prepared to face certain facts, 'I'm not prepared to leave my... our baby to someone else. I've met so many people who've had troublesome nannies...'

'There are lots of good ones about too.'

'I'm sure there are, but it seems such a risk.'

'Well, it would be up to you entirely, but you know, I've had a thought. I've been thinking a lot in the last few days, and I wondered, this area could possibly support a small exclusive dress shop. What would you say? I could subsidise you till you got on your feet, and——'

'James,' her voice was low and thoughtful, 'what a perfectly marvellous idea!'

'You have all the right contacts, don't you?'

'Yes.' The green eyes shone with excitement. 'And you know that rather nice barn right on the drive behind the house? Have you ever thought what a lovely setting that could be for sophisticated country clothes?'

'No,' he answered carefully, 'I confess I hadn't thought of it.'

'I can just imagine a dress shop in a place like that—and oh, James,' Jane clasped her hands together, 'I wouldn't mind having a nanny so much if I were more or less on the premises to keep an eye on our baby.'

'Sounds as if you've got it all worked out. I'm sure you'll make a great success of it.'

'You're laughing at me, aren't you?' Then when he went on to do just that, she joined in till she was forced to wipe away some tears. 'I didn't mean I was going to start next week,' she tried to be dignified and repressive, but didn't quite manage to subdue the smile that would keep coming, 'but it's something to think about, to plan for. Jane Barnard Fashions.' She wrinkled her nose. 'No, not enough zing for what I have in mind, but I've lots of time to come up with a name with some style.'

'Now come on!' James began opening up the various containers from the hamper. 'I'm sure you must be starving—I know I am. There's roast pheasant, potato salad, ham if you prefer that...'

So they ate, smiling at each other, each fascinated by every detail of the other, Jane knowing she was happier than she had ever been in her life before, and that forced her at last to speak.

'James?' Her voice was dreamy, romantic.

'Mmm?' His eyes were caressing, promising.

'Do you think——' Her fingers linked round the slender stem of the glass. She stared down into the golden liquid, surprised that she had lost all taste for it, yet delighted it had given her such a wonderful idea. She couldn't resist a provocative glance from the screen of her long dark lashes. 'Do you think, if I were to pour this wine over you, would there be any reaction, do you imagine?'

He rose to his feet quite slowly, his eyes never leaving hers while he came round the table. He pulled her up and against him with such force that only her toes stayed on the ground, so close that she could hear the fevered beat of his heart merge with her own. 'You know, don't you,' he pressed her head into his shoulder and spoke against her cheek, 'you *know* I have this bargain with myself, a contract that says I must give you time. I've sworn to take it slowly, not to rush you, I want you to enjoy the courtship...'

'Ssh!' There was just enough space for her to breathe, to whisper against his throat. 'Didn't I fall in love with you, James Barnard, when you were impetuous and selfish and...what I'm really saying is, that's enough courtship for the time being.'

She heard his indrawn breath, then he held her away for a moment and stared down at her, his features relaxing into something close to a smile. And with infinite care he swung her up into his arms, walked across the room, through the hall, and began to mount the stairs.

It was late in the afternoon and the wintry sun was fading when Jane woke, stretched drowsily, realised she was in a strange bed and turned her head sharply on the pillow, at once finding herself the subject of a long concentrated study. 'Oh, James...!'

'You sound surprised.' He was lazily indulgent. 'Were you expecting someone else?'

'No, you're my number one choice.' Slightly tentatively she reached out her fingers for his. 'James.'

'Jane?'

'Nothing,' she shook her head. 'Just James.' They smiled at each other in a special and exclusive way. Then, 'Do you think your friend, the one who's selling the house, do you think he'll mind this..this illicit use of his bed?'

'It's your bed.' His hand came out to brush a strand of hair back from her eyes. 'Your bed, your house, your everything. He wanted to sell it as it stood, complete with furniture, and I took a chance on you approving. But if there's anything you want to change . . .'

'I don't. I love the house and everything about it—it's pretty well perfect.'

'And that little room, the one with nothing in it, that's the nursery. You can let yourself go on that.'

'Mmm.' For a few moments Jane thought dreamily about Jemima Puddleduck wallpaper and matching duvet, but was distracted when she felt a finger flick at one of her earrings.

'Do you remember,' James's voice was lazy, totally relaxed and indulgent, 'when someone asked Marilyn Monroe what she wore in bed, do you remember what she said?'

'I've a feeling you're going to tell me.'

'She said she wore Chanel No 5.'

'Good for Marilyn!'

'Well, following on from that, tell me, do you always wear earrings to bed?' Again he flicked a finger at the tiny silver cages.

'Only these ones. You see, they were a present from my lover and I can't bear to be parted from them. Sadly, I don't think I ever thanked him properly.'

'No—well,' even in the darkening room it was possible to recognise the glint of mischief in his eyes, 'I'm sure if you want to do that now, you'll find he's happy to meet you more than halfway.'

4 FREE

Romances
and 2 FREE gifts
just for you!

You can enjoy all the
heartwarming emotion of true love for FREE!
Discover the heartbreak and the happiness, the emotion and
the tenderness of the modern relationships in
Mills & Boon Romances.

We'll send you 4 captivating Romances as a special offer from
Mills & Boon Reader Service, along with the chance to have
6 Romances delivered to your door each month.

Claim your FREE books and gifts overleaf...

An irresistible offer from Mills & Boon

Here's a personal invitation from Mills & Boon Reader Service, to become a regular reader of Romances. To welcome you, we'd like you to have 4 books, a CUDDLY TEDDY and a special MYSTERY GIFT absolutely FREE.

Then you could look forward each month to receiving 6 brand new Romances, delivered to your door, postage and packing free! Plus our free Newsletter featuring author news, competitions, special offers and much more.

This invitation comes with no strings attached. You may cancel or suspend your subscription at any time, and still keep your free books and gifts.

It's so easy. Send no money now. Simply fill in the coupon below and post it to -
Reader Service, FREEPOST, PO Box 236, Croydon, Surrey CR9 9EL.

NO STAMP REQUIRED

Free Books Coupon

Yes! Please rush me 4 free Romances and 2 free gifts! Please also reserve me a Reader Service subscription. If I decide to subscribe I can look forward to receiving 6 brand new Romances each month for just £10.20, postage and packing free. If I choose not to subscribe I shall write to you within 10 days - I can keep the books and gifts whatever I decide. I may cancel or suspend my subscription at any time. I am over 18 years of age.

Ms/Mrs/Miss/Mr _____   EP31R

Address _____

_____

Postcode _____ Signature _____

The truth often hurts . . .

Sometimes it heals

Critically injured in a car accident, Liz Danvers insists her family read the secret diaries she has kept for years – revealing a lifetime of courage, sacrifice and a great love. Liz knew the truth would be painful for her daughter Sage to face, as the diaries would finally explain the agonising choices that have so embittered her most cherished child.

Available now priced £4.99

W❀RLDWIDE

Available from Boots, Martins, John Menzies,
W.H. Smith and other paperback stockists.

Also available from Mills and Boon Reader Service,
P.O. Box 236, Thornton Road, Croydon, Surrey CR9 3RU

Next Month's Romances

Each month you can choose from a wide variety of romance with Mills & Boon. Below are the new titles to look out for next month, why not ask either Mills & Boon Reader Service or your Newsagent to reserve you a copy of the titles you want to buy — just tick the titles you would like and either post to Reader Service or take it to any Newsagent and ask them to order your books.

Please save me the following titles:	Please tick	√
AN OUTRAGEOUS PROPOSAL	Miranda Lee	
RICH AS SIN	Anne Mather	
ELUSIVE OBSESSION	Carole Mortimer	
AN OLD-FASHIONED GIRL	Betty Neels	
DIAMOND HEART	Susanne McCarthy	
DANCE WITH ME	Sophie Weston	
BY LOVE ALONE	Kathryn Ross	
ELEGANT BARBARIAN	Catherine Spencer	
FOOTPRINTS IN THE SAND	Anne Weale	
FAR HORIZONS	Yvonne Whittal	
HOSTILE INHERITANCE	Rosalie Ash	
THE WATERS OF EDEN	Joanna Neil	
FATEFUL DESIRE	Carol Gregor	
HIS COUSIN'S KEEPER	Miriam Macgregor	
SOMETHING WORTH FIGHTING FOR	Kristy McCallum	
LOVE'S UNEXPECTED TURN	Barbara McMahon	

If you would like to order these books in addition to your regular subscription from Mills & Boon Reader Service please send £1.70 per title to: Mills & Boon Reader Service, P.O. Box 236, Croydon, Surrey, CR9 3RU, quote your Subscriber No:.......................................
(If applicable) and complete the name and address details below. Alternatively, these books are available from many local Newsagents including W.H.Smith, J.Menzies, Martins and other paperback stockists from 12th February 1993.

Name:...

Address:...

....Post Code:...........................

To Retailer: If you would like to stock M&B books please contact your regular book/magazine wholesaler for details.